Cyborgs' Origin

BioCircuit Nexus, Volume 0

Aurelia Skye and Juno Wells

Published by Amourisa Press, 2024.

---

1. http://kittunstall.com/newsletter/

Blurb

DR. SIMONE WILEY ALWAYS knew she would inherit her father's colony on the edge of the galaxy, but she never anticipated the depth of challenges—and emotions—that would come with it. Determined to advance her father's legacy of cybernetic research, Simone finds herself working alongside a loyal team of mercenaries led by the imposing yet captivating Tiberius.

When the ruthless Sventian Scourge, led by Vorn, a pieced-together alien with illegal cybernetic enhancements, launches a devastating attack, the colony is thrown into chaos. Tiberius is gravely injured defending the colony, and Simone makes a desperate decision to save him using her groundbreaking technology. Transforming him into the first cyborg, she saves his life because she can't imagine living without him.

As Tiberius adjusts to his new identity, their bond deepens, and they fortify the colony's defenses against the Scourge. It's a matter of when, not if, they'll return, since Vorn wants revenge for Simone shooting him—and he wants her technology. He has no problem killing her to get it.

Cyborgs' Origin *is a passionate and thrilling prequel set a century before the BioCircuit Nexus series, exploring the origins of a love story that will shape a new era.*

Chapter 1—Simone

THE SHUTTLE HUMMED with a steady thrum as it cut through the inky blackness of space. Simone gazed out the viewport, mesmerized by the brilliant tapestry of stars that stretched endlessly before her. A sense of wonder and anticipation filled her, tempered by a tinge of melancholy for the life she was leaving behind.

Turning away from the viewport, her gaze fell on Izzy, who sat across from her, engrossed in the data streaming across her tablet. Izzy's brow furrowed in concentration, her nimble fingers tapping away at the screen. Simone smiled at the sight of her oldest friend, a constant companion through the twists and turns of their academic journey.

"You know, we're supposed to be enjoying the view, not working," Simone teased, her voice tinged with affection.

Izzy glanced up, her expressive brown eyes sparkling behind her rectangular glasses. "Just reviewing the latest schematics for the neural interface. I want to hit the ground running when we arrive." She set aside the tablet, a wry smile playing on her lips. "But you're right. We should savor the moment."

Simone nodded, her thoughts drifting to the ambitious endeavor that awaited them on Durmox C7—her father's legacy, and now hers to steward. "I can't believe we're finally here, on the cusp of realizing my father's dream."

Izzy's expression softened. "He'd be proud of you, Simone. You've poured your heart and soul into this project, just as he did."

A pang of nostalgia tugged at her heart as she thought of her father, the brilliant scientist, whose passion for discovery had inspired her own. "I wish he could see what we're about to accomplish," she said wistfully.

Izzy reached across the aisle, giving Simone's hand a reassuring squeeze. "He's not here physically, but his spirit lives on in this endeavor. We'll make him proud."

Simone returned the gentle pressure, drawing strength from her friend. "You're right, and we have an incredible opportunity ahead of us to push the boundaries of what's possible and to unlock the secrets of the human mind and body through cybernetics. Just imagine the possibilities, Izzy. Restoring lost limbs, enhancing cognitive abilities, and even extending the human lifespan. We're on the precipice of a revolution that could change everything."

Izzy nodded, her expression mirroring Simone's enthusiasm. "And to think, we'll be doing it all on a virgin planet, free from the constraints and bureaucracy that plagued our work back home."

Simone's lips curved into a smile. "Exactly. No more red tape and no more fighting for funding or resources. Just us, our team, and the freedom to explore the depths of human potential."

She leaned back in her seat, allowing the weight of their mission to settle over her. "Of course, there will be challenges. It won't be easy, but if we can do it."

Izzy chuckled, her eyes sparkling with mischief. "If anyone can pull it off, it's you. I'm just along for the ride, making sure you don't get too caught up in your experiments to remember to eat and sleep."

Simone laughed, the sound ringing out in the confines of the shuttle. "Fair point. I'll need you to keep me grounded, as always."

As the shuttle drew nearer to their destination, a surge of anticipation coursed through her veins. This was the beginning of a new chapter, a chance to forge a legacy that would echo through the ages. With Izzy by her side and a world of possibilities awaiting them, she was ready to embrace the unknown and unlock the secrets of the human mind, one groundbreaking discovery at a time.

The shuttle's descent through Durmox C7's atmosphere was smooth, the viewports offering tantalizing glimpses of the verdant world that would soon become Simone's new home. As the craft broke through the cloud cover, her breath caught at the lush tapestry of emerald forests stretching as far as the eye could see, punctuated by towering mountain ranges and shimmering bodies of water.

Izzy leaned closer, her nose nearly pressed against the viewport. "It's even more beautiful than the simulations," she said, clearly awestruck.

Simone could only nod in agreement, her heart swelling with excitement. This was it—the culmination of years of planning and preparation. A world untouched by human hands, a blank canvas upon which they would paint the future of scientific discovery.

The shuttle touched down with a gentle thump, and Simone rose from her seat, smoothing her hands over the crisp lines of her utilitarian jumpsuit. Izzy fell into step beside her as the hatch hissed open, and they descended the ramp, their boots crunching against the reddish soil.

A small contingent awaited them, a group of figures clad in combat gear—the mercenary team her father had hired to provide security for the fledgling colony. Simone's gaze was immediately drawn to the towering figure at the forefront, a man whose very presence seemed to command respect and attention.

He stepped forward, his movements fluid and purposeful, and offered a crisp salute. "Dr. Wiley, welcome to Durmox C7. I'm Tiberius Peña, commander of the Iron Wolves mercenary team."

Simone was momentarily tongue-tied, captivated by the man's rugged features and piercing gaze. She cleared her throat, willing herself to maintain her composure. "Commander Peña, it's a pleasure to meet you." Her voice emerged steadier than she had anticipated, much to her relief.

Tiberius gestured to the others assembled behind him. "Allow me to introduce my team." One by one, he called out their names and roles, each mercenary offering a respectful nod or salute in greeting.

As the introductions concluded, Tiberius turned his attention back to Simone. "We've established a temporary base camp to the east, but our primary objective has been securing the perimeter and ensuring the area is safe for your research endeavors." His expression grew somber. "I won't mince words, Dr. Wiley. This planet is untamed and far from uninhabited. We've encountered several hostile lifeforms, some of which possess formidable defensive capabilities."

Simone's brow furrowed with concern. "What sort of lifeforms are we dealing with?"

Tiberius gestured for one of his team members to step forward—a wiry man with a shock of fiery red hair. "Kian, if you would?"

The mercenary nodded, launching into a detailed account of the various creatures they had encountered thus far, complete with vivid descriptions and strategic assessments. Simone was hanging on his every word, her mind already whirring with potential scientific applications and avenues for further study.

As Kian's accounting drew to a close, Tiberius fixed Simone with an intense gaze. "I trust you understand the risks, Dr. Wiley. This planet may hold boundless potential, but it's also rife with dangers we're prepared to face head-on."

Simone met his stare, her jaw set. "I appreciate your candor, Commander, and rest assured, I have no intention of underestimating the challenges that lie ahead." She paused, her gaze sweeping over the assembled mercenaries. "With a team like yours at our side, I'm confident we can overcome any obstacle."

A ghost of a smile tugged at Tiberius's lips, and Simone felt an unexpected flutter in her chest—a reaction she swiftly tamped down, reminding herself of her aversion to romantic entanglements. Now was not the time for such distractions when she had a mission.

Pushing aside her wayward thoughts, she turned to Izzy, who had been observing the exchange with a knowing glint in her eye. "Shall we get to work, Dr. Chen? We have a colony to build."

Izzy grinned, her expression one of eager anticipation. "Lead the way, Dr. Wiley."

As they fell into step behind Tiberius and his team, Simone stole a glance at the mercenary commander's broad shoulders and confident stride. Despite her best efforts, she was inexplicably drawn to the man, his presence igniting a spark of intrigue she couldn't quite extinguish.

Shaking her head, she forced her attention back to the task at hand. There would be time enough to figure out Tiberius Peña—for now, she had a world to conquer, one groundbreaking discovery at a time.

THE CAVERNOUS CHAMBER echoed with the hum of machinery and the soft murmurs of Simone and Izzy as they worked in tandem, assembling the intricate components of their laboratory. Simone's fingers danced across the control panels, inputting a dizzying array of commands and calibrations, while Izzy deftly maneuvered the robotic arms, guiding them with practiced precision.

"Hand me the neural interface coupler, would you?" Simone's voice cut through the ambient noise, her tone clipped and focused.

Without missing a beat, Izzy plucked the requested component from the nearby workbench and passed it to Simone. Their movements were fluid, honed by years of collaboration and an almost telepathic understanding of each other's needs.

As Simone integrated the coupler into the system, her mind raced with the possibilities that lay before them. This laboratory would be the birthplace of discoveries that could reshape the very fabric of human existence.

"You know," said Izzy, her tone conversational as she monitored the data streams flickering across the holographic displays, "When we were kids, playing mad scientists in your dad's lab, I never imagined we'd end up here—on the cusp of unlocking the secrets of the human mind itself."

A wistful smile tugged at Simone's lips as she recalled those carefree days, when the world had seemed so much simpler. "Neither did I," she said, her gaze lingering on the sleek, state-of-the-art equipment that surrounded them, "But here we are, poised to make history."

Izzy chuckled, her eyes sparkling. "You always did have a flair for the dramatic, Simone."

She arched an eyebrow in mock indignation. "I prefer to think of it as a healthy sense of ambition."

The arrival of Tiberius interrupted their playful banter, his imposing figure filling the doorway. Simone's breath caught, an involuntary reaction she swiftly suppressed.

"Dr. Wiley, Dr. Chen." He greeted them with a curt nod. "I trust the laboratory setup is proceeding smoothly?"

Regaining her composure, Simone straightened, her demeanor shifting to one of professionalism. "Indeed, Commander. We're making excellent progress."

Tiberius's gaze swept over the array of equipment, his expression inscrutable. "I'm intrigued by the nature of your research. Care to enlighten me?"

Simone exchanged a glance with Izzy, silently seeking her friend's approval. At Izzy's subtle nod, she turned back to Tiberius. "Of course, Commander. Our primary focus is the integration of biological and synthetic components—a field known as cybernetics."

Tiberius's brow creased, and Simone found his attentiveness oddly endearing.

"The human body is a remarkable machine, capable of feats that defy our current understanding of biology, but it's also fragile, susceptible to injury, disease, and the ravages of time. What if we could enhance it? Augment its capabilities while preserving its essence?"

As she spoke, Simone gestured to the holographic schematics that hovered before them of intricate diagrams depicting the intricate interplay of organic and synthetic components. "Imagine a world where lost limbs could be restored, not with crude prosthetics, but with fully functional replacements, seamlessly integrated into the body's neural pathways. Where cognitive abilities could be enhanced, allowing us to process information at speeds far beyond our current limitations."

Izzy's enthusiasm mirrored Simone's. "And that's just the beginning. With the right advancements in biocompatible materials and energy sources, we could potentially extend the human lifespan indefinitely, or even achieve a form of cybernetic immortality."

Tiberius's expression remained impassive, but Simone detected a flicker of interest in his eyes. "Ambitious goals, to be sure, but what about the ethical implications? Tampering with the fundamental nature of humanity? Isn't that a line we shouldn't cross?"

Simone nodded, her expression growing somber. "A valid concern, Commander, and one we've grappled with extensively, but I would argue that our work isn't about tampering with humanity but about enhancing it and unlocking our full potential."

She gestured to the laboratory around them, her voice taking on a reverent tone. "This isn't just a place of scientific discovery. It's about our species' insatiable drive for progress. We're not seeking to create something unnatural. We're simply harnessing the tools at our disposal to push the boundaries of what it means to be human."

Tiberius remained silent for a moment, his gaze thoughtful. Finally, he inclined his head in a gesture of respect. "Your passion is admirable, Dr. Wiley. I can't claim to fully understand the intricacies of your work, but I respect your commitment to advancing the human condition."

Warmth bloomed in Simone's chest at his validation that she hadn't realized she craved until that moment. "Thank you, Commander," she said, her voice thick with emotion.

As Tiberius took his leave, she watched his retreating form, her mind whirring with a newfound appreciation for the man's depth and complexity. And his fine ass molded by his tightfitting body armor...

Izzy's voice broke through her reverie, laced with gentle teasing. "You know, for someone who claims to be averse to romantic entanglements, you're certainly making eyes at our stoic mercenary commander."

Her cheeks flushed, but she met Izzy's gaze with a defiant tilt of her chin. "Don't be ridiculous," she scoffed, though her protest lacked conviction. "I was simply appreciating his open-mindedness."

Izzy's answering grin was positively impish. "Of course, Simone. Whatever you say. I suppose his open-mindedness is stored in his ass?"

Shaking her head, Simone turned her attention back to the task at hand, determined to immerse herself in the intricacies of their work, but try as she might, a part of her couldn't quite banish the image of Tiberius's intense gaze, or the way his presence seemed to command the very air around him. With a silent sigh, she pushed aside those errant thoughts, refocusing her mind on the groundbreaking discoveries that awaited them.

IN THE DAYS THAT FOLLOWED, Simone and Izzy fell into a rhythm, their days consumed by the intricate dance of scientific exploration. The laboratory hummed with activity, a hive of intellectual curiosity and cutting-edge technology.

As they delved deeper into the intricacies of cybernetics, Simone was captivated by the sheer scope of the possibilities that lay before them. Each breakthrough, and each incremental step forward, only fueled her determination to push the boundaries of what was achievable.

"Izzy, take a look at these neural interface readings," Simone called out with excitement several weeks after their arrival.

Izzy hurried over, her eyes widening as she took in the data streaming across the holographic display. "Are those what I think they are?"

Simone nodded, barely containing a giddy laugh of triumph. "If I'm interpreting these readings correctly, we've achieved a seamless integration between the synthetic components and the brain's neural pathways."

Izzy's lips curved into a broad grin. "Do you realize what this means? We're one step closer to unlocking the full potential of cybernetic enhancements."

Simone mirrored her friend's elation, her heart pounding with the thrill of discovery. "Exactly. With this level of integration..."

As they delved into the data, dissecting each nuance and implication, Simone was transported to a realm of pure intellectual exhilaration. This was the essence of scientific exploration, the pursuit of knowledge that could reshape the very fabric of human existence.

In the midst of their fervent discussions, the door to the laboratory slid open, admitting Tiberius. Simone's stomach fluttered with anticipation, a reaction she had grown accustomed to suppressing in the mercenary commander's presence.

"Commander." She greeted him with a warm smile, her cheeks flushed with the excitement of their latest breakthrough—and his proximity. "Impeccable timing, as always."

Tiberius arched an inquisitive brow, his gaze flickering between Simone and Izzy. "I take it your research is progressing favorably?"

Izzy beamed, her enthusiasm infectious. "See for yourself, Commander." With a few deft keystrokes, she projected the neural interface readings onto the main display, the intricate data streams dancing across the holographic surface.

As Tiberius leaned in to study the information, Simone was captivated by the intensity of his focus, and the way his brow furrowed ever so slightly as he absorbed the implications of their discovery.

"Remarkable," he said.

Clearing her throat, she forced herself to maintain her composure. "We've achieved a level of integration between synthetic components and the brain's neural pathways that was previously thought impossible."

Tiberius's gaze met hers, his eyes lit with genuine interest. "And the applications of such a breakthrough?"

Simone had a surge of pride, tempered by a sense of humility in the face of the vast unknown that still lay before them. "Potentially limitless, making all the things we previously discussed possible."

A flicker of emotion passed across Tiberius's features, too fleeting for Simone to decipher. "Interesting," he said.

Before Simone could respond, Izzy spoke, her tone tinged with gentle teasing. "Simone's never been one to think small. She likes things *big*."

Simone shot her friend a playful glare, but her heart wasn't truly in it. She was riding the crest of scientific discovery, and nothing could dampen her spirits.

Her cheeks flushed a moment later when Tiberius suddenly shifted, looking uncertain. Without thought, her gaze went to his front, which was amply protected against damage, thus denying her a peek to assuage her curiosity about just how big the commander might be.

When she looked up, she met his gaze. He seemed amused and aroused as he nodded to her. As Tiberius excused himself to leave them to their work, Simone watched his retreating form with appreciation. Beneath his gruff exterior, she had glimpsed a glimmer of intellectual curiosity, a hunger for knowledge that resonated deeply within her.

As if she was just interested in his mind. Even she couldn't fool herself into believing that. Despite her embargo on romance, her thoughts and attraction to the strong merc were leading her astray.

Turning back to Izzy, she was met with a knowing smirk. "What?" she asked, her tone defensive.

Izzy held up her hands in a placating gesture. "Nothing. Just observing the way you light up whenever our stoic commander graces us with his presence."

Simone scoffed, but the heat in her cheeks betrayed her. "Don't be ridiculous."

Izzy's answering grin was positively impish. "It's okay to have a fuck toy and a life outside of the lab, Sim."

Shaking her head and refusing to answer, Simone turned her attention back to the data before them, determined to lose herself in the intricacies of their research. Try as she might, she couldn't quite banish the image of Tiberius's hard body, or her curiosity about how he might taste if she kissed him.

THE SOFT GLOW OF THE evening sun filtered through the panoramic windows, casting a warm, inviting ambiance over the private dining alcove. Simone smoothed her hands over the crisp fabric of her pantsuit, an uncharacteristic flutter of nerves stirring within her. This was just a monthly debriefing and nothing more. There was no reason to feel nervous.

"You've got this, Wiley," she said under her breath, willing herself to maintain her composure.

The door slid open with a hushed hiss, and Tiberius stepped into the room, his imposing figure seeming to command the very space around him. Simone's pulse quickened. "Commander." She nodded, rising from her seat with a welcoming smile.

Tiberius inclined his head, his gaze sweeping over her with an intensity that sent a shiver down her spine. "Dr. Wiley," he said, his voice a rich baritone that resonated to her core.

Gesturing toward the table, she fought to maintain her composure. "Please, have a seat. I took the liberty of selecting a few dishes from the synthicator. I hope you don't mind."

As Tiberius settled into the chair opposite her, Simone admired the fluid grace of his movements and the way his muscles rippled beneath the sleek lines of his combat fatigues. She wondered how he'd move in other...horizontal positions. Her mouth went dry at the thought.

"Not at all," he said, his tone betraying no hint of the effect his presence had on her. "I appreciate the effort."

Silence descended between them, thick and charged with an undercurrent of tension she found both exhilarating and unnerving. She busied herself with pouring them each a glass of wine, her fingers trembling ever so slightly as she handed one to Tiberius.

Their gazes met, and she was momentarily lost in the depths of his warm brown eyes, so intense and yet inscrutable. She cleared her throat, willing herself to regain her composure.

"I wanted to thank you again for your support, Commander," she said, her voice steadier than she had anticipated in light of the way her mind was flitting about. "Your team's presence has been invaluable for our safety and my peace of mind."

He regarded her over the rim of his glass, his expression unreadable. "It's our duty, Dr. Wiley, but I must admit, this mission has been...enlightening."

Simone arched an inquisitive brow. "Oh? How so?"

A ghost of a smile tugged at the corners of his lips, softening the hard planes of his features. "I've witnessed many scientific endeavors in my time, but none quite as ambitious—or as potentially groundbreaking—as yours."

Pride swelled within Simone's chest. "We've barely scratched the surface, Commander, but I won't deny the thrill of standing on the precipice of something truly extraordinary."

Tiberius leaned forward, his elbows resting on the table as he regarded her with an intensity that set her heart racing. "Tell me more," he said, his voice low and compelling.

Simone was drawn in by his rapt attention, her words tumbling forth in a torrent of passion and conviction. As she spoke, she gestured animatedly, lit with the fire of intellectual passion, and through it all, Tiberius remained a captive audience, his expression one of genuine interest and engagement.

When she finally fell silent, breathless and flushed with the exhilaration of her own fervor, he smiled at her.

"Your passion is inspiring, Dr. Wiley," he said, his voice smoky, and she doubted he meant her scientific passion.

A flush bloomed in her cheeks, a reaction she swiftly tamped down as she awkwardly tried to redirect. "I could say the same of you, Commander. Your dedication to your team and this mission is truly remarkable."

Tiberius's expression grew somber, his brow furrowing ever so slightly. "I won't lie to you, Dr. Wiley. My path hasn't been an easy one, but it's forged me into the man I am today, for better or worse."

Simone leaned forward, her eyes alight with curiosity. "Would you share your story with me, Commander? If you're comfortable, that is."

For a moment, he seemed to hesitate, his gaze flickering with an emotion Simone couldn't quite decipher. Then, with a barely perceptible nod, he began to speak. His voice was low and measured, each word carefully chosen as he wove the tale of his childhood on a harsh, lawless fringe planet. Simone was hanging on his every utterance, captivated by the vivid imagery he conjured, the raw honesty with which he laid bare the struggles and hardships he had endured.

As he spoke of joining the local militia, of rising through the ranks and eventually forming the Iron Wolves, Simone admired the strength that had carried him through even the darkest of times. When his tale drew to a close, Simone was regarding him with new understanding.

"You've endured more than most could ever imagine, Commander," she said, her voice thick with emotion. "And yet, here you are, full of strength and integrity."

Tiberius's gaze met hers, his expression unguarded in a way she had never witnessed before. "It's not a path I would wish upon anyone," he said, his voice tinged with vulnerability that tugged at her heartstring, "But it's shaped me into the man I am today—for better or worse."

Without thinking, she reached across the table, resting her hand atop his in a gesture of comfort and solidarity. "For better, Commander," she said firmly. "Undoubtedly, for better."

Tiberius's fingers curled around hers, his touch sending a jolt of electricity through her veins. For a long moment, they remained like that, their gazes locked, the world around them fading into insignificance.

It was Tiberius who finally broke the spell, his hand slipping from hers as he cleared his throat. "Thank you, Dr. Wiley," he said, his voice thick with an emotion Simone couldn't quite place. "For listening...understanding."

Simone nodded, her heart still thundering in her chest. "Of course, Commander. I'm honored that you chose to share your story with me."

As the evening wore on, their conversation ebbed and flowed, touching on topics both profound and mundane. Simone was captivated by Tiberius's intellect, his dry wit, and the unexpected depths that lay beneath his gruff exterior.

Through it all, she was painfully aware of the undercurrent of attraction that simmered between them, a magnetic pull that grew stronger with each passing moment. She was studying the hard planes of his features, the way his eyes crinkled at the corners when he smiled, and the rich timbre of his voice that seemed to reverberate through her very soul and between her legs.

By the time their meal drew to a close, Simone felt as though she had glimpsed a side of Tiberius that few others had ever witnessed, igniting a spark of connection she couldn't extinguish and didn't want to.

As they rose from the table, Simone was reluctant for the evening to end, a part of her yearning to prolong their time together.

He seemed to sense her hesitation, his gaze holding hers with an intensity that sent her pulse fluttering. "Thank you for a wonderful evening, Dr. Wiley," he said, his voice low and intimate. "It's been...enlightening, to say the least."

Her cheeks flushed. "The pleasure was all mine, Commander," she said, feeling awkward.

For a heartbeat, they lingered, the air charged with an electric tension that crackled between them. Then, with a slight incline of his head, Tiberius turned and strode from the room, his departure leaving a tangible absence in his wake.

Simone remained rooted to the spot, her mind whirling with a tumult of emotions. Desire, intrigue, and a deeper curiosity than even the most interesting scientific inquiry could inspire all swirled within her, leaving her breathless and unmoored.

As she made her way back to her quarters, she was replaying the evening's events, savoring each moment, each stolen glance, and each tantalizing glimpse into Tiberius Peña.

She had crossed a threshold with him, and there was no turning back from the path she had set upon. For better or worse, she was inexorably drawn to the mercenary commander, her scientific curiosity blurring with a deeper, more primal yearning she could no longer deny.

As she drifted off to sleep, her dreams were filled with visions of the future, of groundbreaking discoveries and uncharted horizons, all inextricably intertwined with the image of Tiberius's intense gaze and the promise of a linking that threatened to utterly consume her.

Chapter 2—Tiberius

TIBERIUS STRODE PURPOSEFULLY down the corridor, his combat boots echoing against the metal floor. Two months had passed since Dr. Simone Wiley's arrival on Durmox C7, and it was time for him to provide her with another full status report on the colony's progress and the challenges they faced. They wouldn't be having that same delightful dinner meeting as two weeks ago, to his regret.

As he approached the central command hub, the automatic doors slid open, revealing Simone hunched over a console, her brow furrowed in concentration. Izzy stood beside her, gesturing animatedly as she explained something on the display.

Tiberius cleared his throat, announcing his presence. Both women turned, Simone's features relaxing into a warm smile that caused a now-familiar flutter in his chest. "Commander Peña, please come in."

He nodded curtly, stepping into the room. "Dr. Wiley, I'm here to update you on our situation." His gaze flickered to Izzy. "If you'd prefer to discuss this privately..."

"Not at all," said Simone, waving a dismissive hand. "Izzy is my closest confidante. Anything you share with me, she'll hear as well."

Inclining his head in acknowledgment, Tiberius launched into a detailed report, outlining the progress made in establishing the colony's infrastructure and the various challenges they'd encountered. He spoke of the scarcity of certain resources, the need for additional personnel in specific areas, and the ever-present threat of hostile encounters with the planet's indigenous lifeforms. So far, all had been primitive without apparent sentience, and they were trying to minimize interactions to reduce the need for violence.

Throughout his briefing, Simone listened intently, her piercing green eyes fixed on him, occasionally nodding or asking insightful questions. Tiberius was captivated by her keen intellect and determination, qualities he deeply admired, but that wasn't the main draw. He wanted her despite their gaping differences.

She'd grown up the pampered daughter of an intergalactic tycoon descended from obscene levels of wealth. No doubt, she'd struggled, but she'd never had that fear of an empty belly and having no idea when there would be food again. She'd never viscerally fought for survival, so what could they possibly have in common?

Sex. The word brought inevitable mental images that he tried to suppress so he could finish his report. A voice in the back of his mind insisted their connection was deeper than just physical, but he was a practical man, with no time for playing what-if or indulging in fantasies.

As he concluded, Simone leaned back, tapping her fingers against the console thoughtfully. "Thank you, Commander. Your assessment has been invaluable." She paused, a slight smile playing on her lips. "However, I think it's time we dispensed with the formalities. Please, call me Simone."

Tiberius blinked, taken aback by her request. In his line of work, maintaining a professional distance was crucial, yet something about Simone's warm demeanor made him want to acquiesce. "Very well, Simone," he said, testing the weight of her name on his tongue.

Her smile broadened, and she inclined her head. "Do you mind if I use your given name?"

"Tiberius," he said, the corners of his mouth twitching upward in a rare display of amusement.

"I'm aware, though I've only heard you called Commander or Titan."

He nodded. "That's my nickname. It's common among soldiers."

"Do you prefer Titan or Tiberius?"

He didn't have to think that over. "I like how you say my name. Real name…" Their gazes locked and held for a sizzling moment as silence lengthened.

"I'm Izzy." Izzy cleared her throat, a mischievous glint in her eyes. "I'm glad we've all been properly introduced."

Simone nodded at Izzy's words and flashed Tiberius what looked like a shy smile. As he held her gaze, he was drawn to the scientist all over again. Simone threatened to undo his iron control in the best way possible, but possibly so catastrophically that he might not recognize himself when it was over.

TIBERIUS STRODE THROUGH the colony's central courtyard, his combat boots crunching on the gravel path. The warm sunlight filtered through the protective bio-dome, a current necessity until terraforming finished creating the ideal living conditions for human life, casting a gentle glow over the lush vegetation that lined the walkways. Despite the tranquil surroundings, his senses remained on high alert, ever vigilant for potential threats.

As he approached the far end of the courtyard, a commotion caught his attention. Izzy's voice rang out, laced with urgency. "Commander. Over here, quickly."

Tiberius quickened his pace, rounding the corner to find Izzy crouched behind a cluster of bushes, her eyes wide with alarm. Simone stood beside her, clutching a data pad tightly against her chest.

"What's the situation?" he demanded, his hand instinctively moving to the plasma rifle slung across his back.

Izzy motioned for him to keep his voice down. "We were conducting a routine survey of the local flora when a pack of kra'va emerged from the undergrowth." She pointed to a nearby clearing where several large, ostrich-like creatures prowled, their sharp beaks and lethal talons glinting in the sunlight.

Tiberius narrowed his eyes, assessing the threat. The kra'va were known for their aggressively territorial behavior, and their formidable claws could easily disembowel an unwary human. He turned to Simone, his jaw set in a grim line. "How many?"

"Six," she whispered, her knuckles whitening as she gripped the data pad tighter. "We managed to retreat without drawing their attention, but they're blocking the path back to the colony."

Nodding curtly, Tiberius unclipped his rifle and chambered a round.

She frowned. "Don't shoot them."

He shook his head. "Wasn't planning to, Simone. Stay behind me and move swiftly. We'll create a diversion and make a break for the main entrance." His gaze locked with hers as he tried to relay his insistence that she follow his commands. "Do exactly as I say please."

Simone's eyes widened slightly, but she gave a nod.

Tiberius motioned for Izzy to take the lead, keeping Simone safely between them. With a flick of his wrist, he activated his comlink, broadcasting a silent alert to the rest of the Iron Wolves. Within seconds, Lance's voice crackled in his earpiece.

"Sitrep, Commander?"

"Kra'va pack in the central courtyard," Tiberius said. "Preparing to engage and extract the civilians. Converge on my position for backup. Our goal is to avoid engagement. If we must, strive for nonlethal. This was their home first."

"Copy that. Brick and I are en route. Hawk's providing overwatch from the north tower."

Tiberius acknowledged the response with a curt nod, his focus shifting back to the task at hand. He raised his rifle, sighting down the barrel as he assessed the best angle of approach. With a subtle hand signal, he motioned for Izzy and Simone to follow, leading them in a wide arc around the clearing.

As they neared the edge of the vegetation, one of the kra'va raised its head, its beady eyes locking onto their movement. It let out a shrill, warbling cry, alerting the rest of the pack.

"Move," Tiberius shouted, breaking into a sprint.

Izzy and Simone followed closely behind, their footfalls muffled by the soft earth as they raced toward the colony's entrance. The kra'va gave chase, their powerful legs propelling them forward with surprising speed.

Tiberius risked a glance over his shoulder, his finger tightening on the trigger of his rifle. With a series of controlled bursts, he unleashed a volley of plasma bolts, forcing the kra'va to scatter momentarily without injuring any.

The main entrance loomed ahead, its reinforced doors standing open, beckoning them to safety. Tiberius ushered Izzy and Simone through, turning to face the approaching kra'va as Lance and Brick rounded the corner, weapons raised.

"Get them inside." Tiberius took up a defensive position.

Lance and Brick laid down a blistering hail of fire, driving the kra'va back. One of the creatures, its hide scorched by plasma burns, broke through the barrage, charging toward Tiberius with its razor-sharp beak extended.

Time seemed to slow as Tiberius tracked the creature's movements, his finger squeezing the trigger in a smooth, controlled motion, suppressing regret that the confrontation had come to this. A single, well-placed shot caught the kra'va in its exposed throat, dropping it to the ground in a thrashing heap.

The rest of the pack retreated, their warbling cries fading into the distance as they disappeared into the dense foliage.

Tiberius lowered his rifle, his chest rising and falling with measured breaths. He turned to find Simone watching him, her expression awe and concern.

"Is everyone all right?" he asked, his gaze sweeping over the group.

Simone nodded, her eyes still locked on his. "Thanks to you," she said, her voice shaking in a way that sent an unfamiliar tremor through Tiberius's battle-hardened frame.

As the adrenaline of the encounter ebbed, he was captivated by Simone's courage in the face of danger. Clearing his throat, he gestured toward the fallen kra'va. "We should retrieve the carcass. No sense in letting it go to waste."

Lance arched an eyebrow, a hint of amusement dancing in his hazel eyes. "Dinner and a show, eh, Commander?"

Tiberius shot his second-in-command a withering look, but the corners of his mouth twitched ever so slightly, betraying his stoic facade.

TIBERIUS WALKED DOWN the reinforced hallway, his mind still buzzing with thoughts of their run-in with the kra'va. The aroma from the feast lingered even days later, a rich blend of roasted meat and earthy herbs that had filled their makeshift dining hall. He glanced at his watch. It was nearly noon.

His comm unit buzzed to life. "Tiberius? This is Simone," she said in an excited voice.

"Dr. Wiley?" he asked as he adjusted his rifle strap instinctively while quickening his pace toward her lab.

"I need to show you something immediately," she said breathlessly. He could hear footsteps hurriedly in motion through her speaker feed before ending abruptly, and then nothing but static cut off communication midsentence.

He was nearly jogging now until reaching another steel door marked simply LAB 7, where sounds within hinted chaotic activity happening inside. He pushed open its heavy frame to reveal Simone.

Tiberius hurried to the lab, his heart pounding with a mix of anticipation and concern. As he pushed open the door, he found Simone hunched over a holographic interface, her eyes bright with excitement.

"Tiberius," she greeted, a wide grin spreading across her face. "I've made a breakthrough with the biocircuit. If I can figure it out, it could propel our research years ahead in just days."

Her enthusiasm was infectious, and Tiberius felt a surge of pride for Simone's dedication to their shared mission. He moved closer to get a better look at the holographic schematics dancing in the air.

Simone gestured animatedly, her fingers manipulating the hologram with deft precision as she explained her findings. "The biocircuit has this remarkable adaptability, Tiberius. It can integrate seamlessly with organic matter, mimicking and enhancing its functionality. If we can harness its potential, we could revolutionize cybernetic advancements."

As she spoke, her eyes sparkled with an intensity that matched the flickering hologram before them. Tiberius marveled at her passion and brilliance, feeling a surge of admiration for her relentless pursuit of knowledge.

"Imagine the possibilities," she continued, her voice vibrant with excitement. "Enhanced prosthetics, neuro-synaptic interfaces, even advanced sensory feedback for cyborgs. This could change everything."

Tiberius nodded in agreement, his mind racing with the implications of Simone's discovery. The potential for integrating the biocircuit into their existing technology was staggering. It could redefine the capabilities of their cybernetic enhancements and offer new opportunities for collaboration between humans and cyborgs.

As Simone delved into the intricate details of her breakthrough, Tiberius marveled at her expertise and dedication to their shared cause. Her relentless pursuit of scientific advancement and her commitment to improving the lives of both humans and cyborgs left him in awe.

He was glad she was their lead researcher. Her passion and determination were good for their mission on Durmox C7, and Tiberius was deeply grateful for her dedication.

With each passing moment, as Simone's words painted a vivid picture of their future possibilities, Tiberius felt a growing sense of optimism and renewed purpose. The prospect of harnessing the biocircuit's potential to bridge the gap between humans and cyborgs ignited a spark of hope within him.

Together, they could usher in a new era of collaboration and progress, one that transcended the boundaries of fear and misunderstanding that had long divided their worlds.

As Simone continued to unravel the intricacies of her breakthrough, Tiberius was struck by the sheer magnitude of her intellect and vision. She was more than just a brilliant scientist.

Tiberius was leaning closer, his gaze locked with Simone's. Her eyes widened slightly, but she didn't pull away. The air seemed to crackle with an electric tension, drawing them together like opposite poles of a magnet.

For a fleeting moment, Tiberius allowed himself to entertain the thought of closing the distance between them. His eyes flickered to Simone's lips, full and inviting, and he imagined how they might feel against his own.

But just as quickly as the impulse arose, he tamped it down, reining in his wayward thoughts. He was a professional, a soldier, and such indulgences were unacceptable—especially with someone as important as Simone.

Clearing his throat, Tiberius took a step back, creating a respectable distance between them once more. "You should get back to your research," he said, his voice gruff but steady. "Your work is invaluable to the colony's success."

Simone blinked, as if emerging from a trance. A faint flush crept up her neck, coloring her cheeks a delicate shade of pink. "Of course," she said, her fingers toying with the edge of the data pad she still clutched.

Tiberius turned on his heel, striding toward the exit with purposeful steps. As he reached the door, he paused, his hand hovering over the control panel. Without looking back, he spoke again, his tone softer than before. "Let me know if you require any assistance, Simone."

With that, he stepped through the doorway, letting it slide shut behind him. Once in the corridor, he exhaled slowly, his shoulders sagging ever so slightly as the tension bled from his frame.

What had come over him back there? He was a seasoned warrior, hardened by years of combat and sacrifice. Yet, in Simone's presence, he was teetering on the edge of vulnerability, his carefully constructed defenses threatening to crumble.

Shaking his head, Tiberius pushed the unsettling thoughts aside and focused on the task at hand. He had a colony to protect, a mission to fulfill. Personal entanglements were a luxury he couldn't afford, no matter how alluring the temptation.

With renewed determination, he set off down the corridor, his boots echoing against the metal floor with each decisive stride.

DAYS PASSED, AND TIBERIUS was drawn back to Lab 7 time and again, each visit fueled by a different pretext. Sometimes it was to discuss security protocols or resource allocation, other times to seek Simone's input on a particular challenge they faced.

Yet, no matter the ostensible reason, Tiberius couldn't deny the undercurrent of anticipation that thrummed through his veins whenever he stepped into the lab. Simone's presence was a magnetic force, pulling him in with an intensity he couldn't quite comprehend.

On one such visit, Tiberius found Simone hunched over a workbench, her brow furrowed in concentration as she tinkered with a complex array of circuitry. Izzy hovered nearby, offering occasional commentary and handing Simone tools as needed.

"What are you working on?" Tiberius asked, his voice cutting through the comfortable silence that had settled over the lab.

Simone glanced up, her eyes brightening as she registered his presence. "Ah, Tiberius," she greeted warmly. "Come, take a look."

She beckoned him closer, and Tiberius was drawn to her side, peering over her shoulder at the intricate components laid out before her. Simone launched into an animated explanation, her words tumbling over one another in her excitement.

As she spoke, Tiberius was captivated not only by the complexity of her work but also by the passion that radiated from her every gesture, every inflection. Her hands danced across the circuitry, deftly manipulating the delicate components with a surgeon's precision.

"...and if we can integrate the biocircuit with our existing cybernetic enhancements, the potential applications are limitless," Simone concluded, her eyes shining with enthusiasm.

Tiberius nodded, his mind whirring as he processed the implications of her words. "It's truly remarkable," he said, his gaze lingering on her face, taking in the sight of her infectious joy.

Simone's lips curved into a warm smile, and for a heartbeat, the world seemed to narrow to the two of them, suspended in a moment of shared wonder and possibility.

Izzy cleared her throat, shattering the fragile spell that had enveloped them. "If you'll excuse me," she said, a knowing glint in her eyes as she gathered her tools. "I'll give you two some space to discuss the finer points."

With a wink and a playful grin, Izzy slipped from the lab, leaving Tiberius and Simone alone in the sudden silence.

Tiberius shifted his weight, acutely aware of the proximity between them. He could feel the warmth of Simone's body, the subtle scent of her shampoo mingling with the crisp, sterile air of the lab.

"Izzy seems to think we require privacy," he remarked, his voice dropping to a low rumble.

Simone's cheeks flushed, but she held his gaze steadily. "Perhaps she's right," she said, her tone tinged with a hint of invitation.

The air grew thick with tension, charged with unspoken possibilities. Tiberius was leaning closer, drawn in by the magnetic pull of Simone's presence.

This time, he didn't fight the impulse.

His hand rose, calloused fingers grazing the silken curve of Simone's cheek. Her eyes fluttered closed at his touch, her lips parting ever so slightly in a silent invitation.

Tiberius's heart thundered in his chest as he closed the final distance between them, his lips capturing Simone's in a searing kiss. She melted into his embrace, her arms winding around his neck as she returned the kiss with equal fervor.

Time seemed to suspend, the world fading away until only the two of them remained, locked in a passionate embrace that shattered the boundaries between them. In that moment, Tiberius felt more alive than he had in years, his soul ignited by the fire that burned between them.

When they finally broke apart, breathless and flushed, Tiberius cradled Simone's face in his hands, his thumbs tracing the delicate curves of her cheekbones.

"Simone," he said, his voice a reverent whisper. "What are we doing?"

She met his gaze, her eyes shimmering with a kaleidoscope of emotions. "Something inevitable," she breathed, her fingers tangling in the short strands at the nape of his neck.

Tiberius searched her face, his heart swelling with a depth of feeling he hadn't dared to acknowledge until now. In that moment, he knew there was no turning back, no retreating behind the walls he had so carefully constructed.

Simone had breached his defenses, laying bare the vulnerability he had sworn to never reveal, and in her arms, he found not weakness, but a strength he had never known—the courage to embrace the beating heart that had been dormant for far too long.

With a low growl, he crushed his lips against hers once more, surrendering to the passion that consumed them both.

Chapter 3—Simone

SIMONE'S HEART RACED as she made her way through the colony's corridors, searching for Tiberius. The past two days had been a whirlwind of conflicting emotions since their unexpected kiss in the lab. At first, she had been elated, the spark between them finally igniting into something more tangible, but as the initial euphoria faded, doubt and uncertainty crept in, leaving her questioning the wisdom of pursuing a relationship with the commander of their mercenary force.

She had thrown herself into her work, burying her feelings beneath a mountain of research and experiments, but even as she pored over data and tinkered with biocircuits, her thoughts kept drifting back to Tiberius—the warmth of his lips against hers and the strength of his arms as he held her close. No matter how hard she tried to focus, she couldn't eliminate the memory of that moment.

Now, after two days of avoidance and internal struggle, Simone had come to a decision. She couldn't let fear and doubt dictate her actions. She needed to confront Tiberius and be honest about her feelings and reservations. It was the only way to move forward, whether that meant exploring their connection further or agreeing to maintain a professional distance.

As she rounded a corner, she spotted Tiberius emerging from the armory, his broad shoulders filling out his combat gear. Her stomach fluttered with nerves, but she squared her shoulders and quickened her pace to catch up with him.

"Tiberius, wait," she called out, her voice echoing in the empty corridor.

He turned, his dark eyes widening slightly as he saw her approaching. "Dr. Wiley. What can I do for you?"

Simone winced at the formal address, a stark reminder of the distance she had put between them over the past two days. She came to a stop before him, her hands fidgeting at her sides as she searched for the right words.

"I... I need to talk to you. About what happened in the lab."

His expression remained neutral, but she could see a flicker of something in his eyes—anticipation, perhaps, or apprehension. He nodded, gesturing for her to continue.

Simone took a deep breath, her heart slamming against her ribs. "I've been avoiding you," she said, the words tumbling out in a rush. "After we kissed, I didn't know how to face you. I was scared of what it meant, of how it might complicate things between us."

Tiberius's lips twitched, a hint of a smile playing at the corners. "I noticed," he said, his deep voice sending a shiver down her spine. "I figured you needed some space to process everything."

She nodded, relieved he understood even without her having to explain. It was one of the things she admired most about him—his ability to read her, to sense what she needed without her having to say a word.

"I did, but I realize now that avoiding you wasn't the answer. We need to talk about this, to figure out what it means for us."

He stepped closer, his presence filling her senses. She could feel the heat radiating off his body and smell the faint scent of gun oil and sweat that clung to his skin. It was intoxicating, and for a moment, she forgot what she had been about to say.

"I'm impressed," he said, his voice low and intimate. "It takes courage to confront something like this head-on."

Simone's cheeks warmed at the praise, a small smile tugging at her lips. "I don't know about courage. More like necessity. I can't keep running from my feelings, no matter how scary they might be."

Tiberius reached out, his calloused fingers brushing against her cheek. The touch sent a jolt of electricity through her, and she leaned into his hand, savoring the contact.

"I'm glad you came to find me," he said softly. "I've been thinking about that kiss too. About what it could mean for us."

Her heart skipped a beat. "And what do you think it means?"

Tiberius's thumb traced the curve of her cheekbone, his eyes searching hers. "I think it means we have something special, something worth exploring, but only if you want to."

She swallowed hard, her mouth suddenly dry. There were a thousand reasons why pursuing a relationship with Tiberius was a bad idea—the power imbalance between them, the potential for distraction from their mission, and the risk of heartbreak if things went wrong—but standing there in that moment, with his hand on her face and his gaze locked on hers, none of those reasons seemed to matter. "I do want to. I'm scared of what it could mean, of how it might change things between us, but I can't deny what I feel for you."

His smile widened, his eyes crinkling at the corners. "Then let's figure it out together," he said, his voice warm with promise. "One step at a time."

Simone nodded, a giddy laugh bubbling up in her throat. She felt lighter than she had in days, the weight of her doubts and fears lifting from her shoulders. "Agreed," she said, rising up on her toes to press a soft kiss to his lips.

As his arms encircled her, drawing her close, she pressed against him. They stayed like that for a long moment, wrapped in each other's arms, the world around them fading away. When they finally pulled apart, she couldn't stop the smile that spread across her face, mirroring the one on his.

"We should probably get back to work," she said reluctantly, glancing down the empty corridor. "People will start to wonder where we are."

Tiberius chuckled, his hand finding hers and giving it a gentle squeeze. "Let them wonder," he said, his eyes twinkling with mischief. "We have more important things to discuss."

Simone raised an eyebrow, curiosity piqued. "Oh? Like what?"

He leaned in closer, his breath warm against her ear. "Like when I can take you out on a proper date," he said, his voice sending a shiver down her spine. "Somewhere away from prying eyes and colony business."

Simone's heart fluttered at the thought, a thrill of anticipation coursing through her. "I'd like that," she said softly, meeting his gaze. "Very much."

Tiberius grinned, his thumb brushing over the back of her hand. "Then it's a date," he said, his voice filled with promise. "I'll make the arrangements and let you know the details."

Simone nodded, excitement bubbling up inside her. "I can't wait," she said, her smile widening, "But for now, we really should get back to work. The colony won't run itself."

Tiberius sighed, a rueful chuckle escaping his lips. "You're right, as always," he said, reluctantly releasing her hand. "Duty calls."

Simone stepped back, already missing his touch, but there would be time for more later, for stolen moments and whispered promises. For now, they had a job to do. "I'll see you later," she said, her voice filled with warmth. "And, Tiberius? Thank you for understanding and being patient with me."

His expression softened, his eyes filled with tenderness. "Always," he said, the word like a vow.

With one last smile, she turned and headed back down the corridor, her steps lighter than they had been in days. She felt like she could take on the world, and that was a feeling worth holding onto, no matter what the future might bring.

The afternoon sun was just beginning to dip below the horizon, casting long shadows across the shipyard, when Simone's comm device chimed with an incoming message from Tiberius, requesting her presence near the docking bays at dusk.

Anticipation and nervousness swirled within her as she hurried to make herself presentable. After freshening up and changing into a simple but flattering sundress, she made her way through the winding corridors, the occasional crew member or scientist offering a polite nod as she passed.

By the time she reached the shipyard, the sky had taken on a warm, amber hue, the twin moons just peeking over the horizon. Tiberius stood waiting beside a sleek, open-topped skid, his expression inscrutable as always. Yet Simone could detect a glimmer of something in his dark eyes—excitement, perhaps, or even a hint of nervousness to match her own.

"You look beautiful," he said, his deep voice sending a shiver down her spine.

Simone felt heat rise to her cheeks at the compliment. "Thank you," she said, suddenly self-conscious under his intense gaze. "Where are we going?"

A faint smile tugged at the corners of Tiberius's mouth. "It's a surprise, but I promise, you'll enjoy it."

Curiosity piqued, Simone climbed into the passenger seat of the skid, inhaling the crisp evening air tinged with the scent of the planet's exotic flora. Tiberius slid into the driver's seat beside her, and with a gentle hum, the skid lifted off the ground, gliding smoothly out of the shipyard and into the dusky landscape beyond.

As they soared over rolling hills and winding rivers, Simone marveled at the breathtaking scenery unfolding before them. The twin moons cast a soft, ethereal glow over the terrain, illuminating the vibrant hues of the alien foliage and the shimmering waters below. She'd been here for months and hadn't taken time to really see anything outside her lab. "It's beautiful."

He took her hand, his calloused fingers intertwining with hers. "Wait until you see our destination," he said, his voice low and intimate.

A thrill of anticipation coursed through Simone at his words, and she leaned back in her seat, content to simply enjoy the journey and the company of the man beside her.

After a short flight, Tiberius guided the skid toward a secluded valley nestled between two towering mountain ranges. As they descended, Simone gasped, her eyes widening at the sight that greeted them.

The valley floor was a riot of color of exotic flora and fauna unlike anything she had ever seen. Towering crystalline trees glittered in the moonlight, their branches swaying gently in the evening breeze. Vibrant, bioluminescent flowers dotted the landscape, their petals unfurling in mesmerizing patterns, and in the distance, a shimmering lake reflected the celestial bodies above, its waters rippling with life.

"Echo Valley," said Tiberius, his voice filled with wonder. "One of the most biodiverse regions on the planet, and a designated conservation zone per your father."

Simone could only nod, rendered speechless by the sheer beauty that surrounded them. As the skid touched down on a grassy knoll, she stepped out, her feet sinking into the soft, moss-like ground. "It's... magnificent," she whispered, turning in a slow circle to take in every detail.

Tiberius moved to stand beside her, his presence warm and reassuring. "I thought you might appreciate a change of scenery," he said, his eyes never leaving her face. "A chance to escape the confines of the colony, if only for a little while."

Simone met his gaze, her heart swelling with affection. "It's perfect," she said, reaching out to take his hand. "Thank you for bringing me here."

His thumb brushed over her knuckles, sending a shiver of pleasure through her. "There's more," he said, a hint of mischief in his voice. He gestured toward a nearby clearing, where a blanket had been spread out with a small picnic basket resting atop it.

Simone laughed, delighted by the thoughtful gesture. "You really did think of everything, didn't you?"

Tiberius's lips curved into a rare, unguarded smile. "I wanted this evening to be special," he said, his voice low and intimate. "A chance for us to be together, away from the demands of the colony and our responsibilities."

Warmth bloomed in Simone's chest at his words, and she stepped closer, drawn to him like a moth to a flame. "It already is," she said, her free hand coming to rest against his chest, feeling the steady beat of his heart beneath her palm.

Tiberius's gaze smoldered, his arm snaking around her waist to pull her flush against him. For a moment, they simply stood there, bodies intertwined, the world around them fading into insignificance. Then, with a tenderness that belied his imposing stature, he cupped Simone's face in his hands and lowered his mouth to hers.

The kiss was a soft, unhurried, gentle exploration of lips and tongues. Simone melted into his embrace, her fingers tangling in the short hair at the nape of his neck as she returned the kiss with equal fervor.

Desire unfurled within her, a slow burn that ignited every nerve ending. She had kissed Tiberius before, in the heat of the moment, but this was different. This was a promise, a declaration of something deeper and more profound than mere physical attraction.

As if sensing the shift, he deepened the kiss, his hands roaming the curves of her body with reverent exploration. She responded in kind, tracing her fingers over the hard planes of his chest and the rippling muscles of his back.

Slowly, almost reluctantly, they broke apart, foreheads resting together as they caught their breath. Her lips curved into a radiant smile. "That was…" she began, trailing off as words failed her.

He chuckled, the sound rich and warm. "It sure was," he said, brushing a stray lock of hair from her face. "Perhaps we should take a moment to enjoy the picnic I've prepared."

She nodded, her cheeks flushed with desire and something more—a sense of rightness, of belonging, that she had never experienced before. As they settled onto the blanket, she leaned into Tiberius's side, savoring the solid warmth of his body against hers.

For a while, they simply sat in comfortable silence, sharing the food and drinks Tiberius had packed, their fingers occasionally brushing in a tantalizing caress. The moons climbed higher in the sky, bathing the valley in their ethereal glow, and Simone was utterly captivated by the beauty that surrounded them.

Yet as breathtaking as the scenery was, she found her gaze continually drawn back to Tiberius, taking in the sharp angles of his face and the intensity of his dark eyes. There was a vulnerability in his expression, a rawness that she had never seen before, and it stirred something deep within her—a need that could no longer be denied.

Slowly, almost unconsciously, she leaned in, her lips seeking his once more. Tiberius met her halfway, his kiss searing, consuming, and igniting a conflagration of desire that threatened to consume them both.

They tumbled to the ground, their bodies entwined, the passion between them burning brighter than the twin moons above. Tiberius's lips trailed a path of fire along her jawline, her throat, her collarbone, and Simone arched into him, her breath coming in ragged gasps.

His hands explored her body, mapping the contours of her curves with exquisite precision, and she writhed beneath him, desperate for more. She tugged at his shirt, realizing this was the first time she'd seen him without body armor, and she liked being this close to his flesh—soon to be bared to her with the removal of the thin T-shirt.

The fabric slid over his head, revealing a landscape of sculpted muscle and smooth skin that made her mouth go dry. She ran her hands over his chest, reveling in the feel of him and gently raking her nails across his nipples, drawing a low growl from deep in his throat.

He pulled her closer, his mouth claiming hers once more as his hands slipped inside her bodice, caressing her breasts through the thin fabric of her bra. She moaned, arching into him as his thumbs brushed against her hardened nipples, sending a jolt of pleasure straight to her throbbing pussy.

She untied the sundress and let it pool at her waist so she could fumble with the clasp of her bra, eager to feel his bare skin against her own, and he helped her remove it, tossing the garment aside. His lips captured one of her nipples, sucking and teasing, and she cried out, bucking her hips against him as she sought friction for her aching center.

His teeth grazed her nipple, and she gasped, head falling back in ecstasy. He moved lower, trailing kisses down her stomach, and she trembled, on fire with need. "Please," she whispered, not even sure what she was asking for, but knowing she needed more.

He obliged, lifting her skirt ot her waist as his tongue darted out to taste her through the fabric of her panties, and she nearly came undone right then. She reached for him, her fingers tangling in his hair as she urged him on, and he chuckled, the sound vibrating against her most sensitive spot and making her whimper.

"So impatient."

He pulled back long enough to completely strip her, removing the sundress and her bra with slow, sensual movements until she lay before him in nothing but a pair of lacy panties. She felt exposed, vulnerable, and yet, she'd never felt more desired.

He gazed at her with such intensity that she might melt under the heat of his stare.

"You're so beautiful, Simone. I've wanted this since the moment I laid eyes on you."

She flushed, her heart pounding as he lowered his head, his tongue tracing a line of fire up her inner thigh. She shuddered, her hips rising to meet him, and he hooked his fingers in the waistband of her panties, pulling them down and exposing her slick folds.

He groaned, the sound sending a fresh wave of arousal through her, and she cried out as his tongue found her clit, swirling around the sensitive nub and driving her wild with pleasure. Her fingers tightened in his hair, holding him against her as he feasted on her pussy, licking and sucking until she was on the verge of coming apart.

Her breath came in ragged gasps, her body trembling as she teetered on the edge of release, and she begged him not to stop, her voice hoarse with desire. "Please, Tiberius, don't stop. I'm so close..."

He hummed against her, the vibration sending her over the edge, and she shattered, her orgasm crashing through her in waves of bliss. She called out his name, her body quaking with the force of her climax, and he continued to lap at her, drawing out her pleasure until she was spent.

When she finally came down from her high, she was boneless and sated, her limbs heavy with satisfaction. Tiberius looked up at her with a smug grin, his face glistening with her juices, and she laughed, her chest heaving as she tried to catch her breath. "You look like you had a feast."

He smirked, leaning in to kiss her, and she tasted herself on his lips, the flavor heady and intoxicating. "I did, and I plan to do it again and again."

Simone shivered at the promise in his words, her body already responding to the thought of more pleasure. Hastily, she helped him disrobe until they were both completely nude. "I want your mouth over and over, but first..." She reached between them to stroke his cock. Her head cleared for a moment, and she asked, "May I scan you?"

He nodded his assent, and she initiated the scan with a discreet press of the button on her wrist comm. In seconds, it assured her he was healthy and astoundingly fertile. She giggled when she showed him. "It's a good thing I have a BioChip. Your sperm count—"

He growled, taking possession of her mouth with his again, kissing her deeply before pulling away. "There are better ways to use your mouth than talking about sperm count." His lips twitched.

She arched a brow. "I've never done that before, but I confess to some scientific curiosity." She squeezed his cock again, making him groan. "I haven't really done much of...this."

His smile was tender. "I thought that might be the case. You're a woman of brains, but I'm the one who unlocked your passionate side." He bent to kiss her again.

She put up a hand. "Do you want to scan me?"

"No, I trust you. I know you wouldn't lie to me like I'd never lie to you. I'm going to make love to you, Simone. I'm going to take my time and show you how a man should treat a woman. I'm going to worship every inch of your body and make you scream my name."

She swallowed hard, her heart pounding at the intensity of his words. "Tiberius, I'm yours. I'm ready for whatever you want to give me."

He kissed her again, slowly and deeply, and she melted into him, her body aching for more. His cock was still in her hand, and she regretfully broke the kiss. "I want to taste you."

He groaned, letting her push him back onto the blanket. She knelt between his legs, taking a moment to admire the sight of his cock, hard and proud, waiting for her.

She licked her lips, then leaned forward to run her tongue along the length of his shaft. He shuddered, gripping the edges of the blanket, and she smiled. She wanted to drive him as crazy as he drove her. She swirled her tongue around the tip of his cock, tasting the salty sweetness of his precum. She moaned, taking more of him into her mouth, and he gasped, bucking his hips involuntarily.

It was definitely strange but not unpleasant. She rather liked it when he rolled his hips. At first, the scientist in her tried to analyze his reactions so she could hone her technique, but soon, she was lost in the sensations. She loved the feel of his cock in her mouth, the way he tasted, and the sounds he made. She sucked and licked, taking him deeper and deeper until his cock hit the back of her throat.

He cried out, his body tensing, and it was clear he was close. She pulled back, releasing his cock from her mouth. She looked down at him, her eyes blazing with desire. "I need you inside me, Tiberius. I can't wait any longer."

He sat up, grabbing her and pulling her into his lap. She straddled him, her thighs on either side of his, and she reached down to guide him into her. She sank down on his cock, taking him fully into her, and they both moaned at the sensation.

He kissed her as he began to move, thrusting up into her. She met his thrusts, her hips moving in perfect rhythm with his. They moved together, their bodies joined as one, and the pleasure was almost unbearable. She clung to him, digging her nails into his shoulders as she rode him, her cries of ecstasy echoing through the valley.

The sound of her voice must have been enough to send him over the edge, and he came with a shout, spilling himself deeply inside her. She followed seconds later, her orgasm crashing over her, and she collapsed against him, spent and sated.

Afterward, they laid together, bodies entwined on the blanket, their limbs intertwined, and hearts beating in perfect synchronicity. She traced idle patterns on his chest, her head pillowed against his shoulder as she savored the intimacy of the moment. "You were amazing."

Tiberius chuckled, the rumble reverberating through his chest. "So were you," he said, pressing a tender kiss to her brow. "Words seem inadequate."

Simone hummed her agreement, snuggling closer to his warmth. She felt utterly content, as though she had finally found the missing piece of herself, the part she hadn't even known was absent until Tiberius had come into her life.

As the moons continued their stately march across the heavens, Simone allowed her eyes to drift shut, secure in the knowledge that whatever the future might hold, she would face it with Tiberius by her side, and in that moment, nothing else mattered.

Chapter 4—Simone

THE NEXT MORNING, SIMONE awoke with a contented smile on her lips, the memories of the previous night still fresh in her mind. She stretched languidly, savoring the delicious ache in her muscles—a reminder of the passionate hours she had spent in Tiberius's arms before they finally roused themselves to return to the colony near dawn.

As she rose from her own bed, she caught sight of herself in the mirror, her cheeks flushing at the sight of the love bites peppering her neck and collarbone. Tiberius had been insatiable, his lips and teeth leaving a trail of marks across her skin, each one a brand of possession that sent a thrill through her.

Dressing quickly, she made her way to the lab, her mind already buzzing with ideas and theories. She couldn't wait to dive back into her work, to lose herself in the intricacies of her research—and yet, a part of her remained tethered to the memories of the night before, her thoughts continually drifting back to Tiberius and the way he had made her feel.

As she entered the lab, she found Izzy already hard at work, her brow furrowed in concentration as she tinkered with one of the diagnostic machines. Simone cleared her throat, and Izzy looked up, her eyes widening as she took in Simone's appearance.

"Hmm..." A sly grin spread across her face. "Someone had a good night."

Simone flushed, her fingers self-consciously tracing the marks on her neck. "Izzy..."

"No need to be embarrassed." Izzy chuckled, waving a dismissive hand. "I'm happy for you, Simone. It's about time you let loose and had some fun."

Simone rolled her eyes, but a smile tugged at her lips. "It was... incredible," she said, her voice dropping to a hushed whisper. "I've never felt anything like that before."

Izzy's expression softened, her eyes shining with genuine warmth. "Love can do that. Makes you feel things you never thought possible."

Simone's breath caught in her throat at the word "love," a sudden fluttering in her chest. Was that what she felt for Tiberius? She had been drawn to him from the moment they met, captivated by his strength, his loyalty, and the depths of compassion that lay beneath his gruff exterior, but love? The thought was both exhilarating and terrifying.

As if sensing her inner turmoil, Izzy reached out to give her hand a reassuring squeeze. "Don't overthink it," she said gently. "Just let yourself feel for once. You deserve to be happy."

She nodded, swallowing past the lump in her throat. Izzy was right. She had spent too long denying herself the simple pleasures of life, too focused on her work and her ambitions to allow herself to truly live, but Tiberius had awakened something within her, a fire that burned brighter than any scientific curiosity, and she could no longer ignore it.

Pushing aside her tumultuous thoughts, she turned her attention to the work at hand, her mind immediately zeroing in on the problem she had been grappling with for weeks. She moved to the central console, her fingers flying across the holographic interface as she pulled up the schematics for the biocircuit interface.

"I've been going over my father's notes again," she said, her brow creasing in concentration, "And I think I might have found a way to power the biocircuits without overloading the system."

Izzy's eyes lit up with interest, and she moved to stand beside Simone, peering over her shoulder at the display. "What did you have in mind?"

Simone took a deep breath, her mind racing as she pieced together the fragments of her epiphany. "We've been trying to draw power directly from the fusion reactor, but the energy output is too volatile. We need a way to regulate the flow and modulate the energy before it reaches the biocircuits."

She tapped a series of commands, and a new set of schematics appeared, this time depicting a complex array of circuits and conduits. "I think we can use a modified version of the energy regulators we developed for the colony's power grid," she said, her voice quickening with excitement. "If we can integrate them into the biocircuit interface, they should be able to handle the raw power from the reactor and distribute it in a controlled, stable manner."

Izzy's eyes widened as she studied the schematics, her mind no doubt already whirring with calculations and potential modifications. "It's brilliant," she said, her gaze meeting Simone's with admiration, "But the regulators were never designed to handle that kind of energy output. We'd have to make some serious adjustments to the circuitry, maybe even incorporate some of the shielding protocols we developed for the mining drills."

Simone nodded, her lips curving into a smile. "Exactly," she said, her eyes sparkling with determination. "It won't be easy, but if we work together, we can make it happen."

Izzy grinned, her excitement mirroring Simone's own. "Well, what are we waiting for?" she asked, rubbing her hands together. "Let's get to work."

For the next several hours, the two women lost themselves in a flurry of calculations, simulations, and prototypes. They worked in tandem, bouncing ideas off each other and fine-tuning their designs with a level of precision that bordered on obsession.

Time seemed to blur, the world around them fading into insignificance as they pursued their goal with single-minded focus. Simone's earlier distractions melted away, replaced by the familiar thrill of scientific discovery, and the rush of adrenaline that came with pushing the boundaries of what was possible.

Finally, after what felt like an eternity, they stepped back from the workbench, their faces flushed with exertion and triumph. Before them sat a sleek, compact device—a fusion of cutting-edge technology and ingenious design, a masterpiece that promised to revolutionize the field of human enhancement.

Simone reached out, her fingers tracing the contours of the device with reverence. "We did it," she said, her voice thick with emotion. "We actually did it."

Izzy slung an arm around her shoulders, her grin wide and infectious. "Of course we did," she said, her tone brimming with pride. "You're brilliant, Simone, and I'm not too shabby myself."

Simone laughed, the sound bubbling up from deeply within her chest, a release of the tension and excitement that had been building all day. In that moment, she felt truly alive, her heart swelling with a sense of accomplishment and possibility.

As she gazed at the device, her mind raced with the implications of their breakthrough, the potential it held for not only their research but for the betterment of humanity as a whole, and yet, beneath it all, she couldn't shake the thought of Tiberius, the memory of his touch, his kiss, and the way he had made her feel like the most cherished, most desired woman in the universe.

Warmth bloomed in her chest, a realization dawning that this—this perfect fusion of scientific discovery and human connection—was what she had been searching for all along. Anything was possible, and the boundaries of what they could achieve were limitless.

Chapter 5—Simone

THE NIGHT SEEMED TRANQUIL as Simone lay beside Tiberius, his muscular arm draped over her waist. His deep, even breaths brushed against her neck, and she savored the warmth of his body next to hers. After months of suppressing her feelings, she had finally surrendered to the undeniable connection between them.

A deafening explosion shattered the stillness, the concussive force rattling the walls. Tiberius bolted upright, his combat instincts kicking in instantly. "Stay down." he said harshly, rolling off the bed and snatching his sidearm from the nightstand.

Simone clutched the sheets to her chest, heart pounding. Through the window, flashes of light illuminated the night sky, followed by more thunderous blasts.

Tiberius pulled on his fatigues, movements swift and precise. "We're under attack. Get dressed quickly." His tone brooked no argument.

As Simone scrambled for her clothes, another explosion rocked the compound, closer this time. She stumbled, catching herself against the wall. "Who's attacking us?"

His expression was grim as he looked at his comm, clearly communicating with one of his mercs. After a minute, he said,

"The Sventian Scourge." He tossed her a laser pistol. "Can you handle this?"

She nodded, her grip firm on the unfamiliar weapon. Together, they raced into the corridor, the air thick with smoke and the acrid smell of scorched metal. Chaos reigned in the command center. Alarms blared, and screens flickered with images of the colony under siege.

Izzy rushed toward them, her face streaked with soot. "Vorn Drekar's forces breached the perimeter. They're hitting us from all sides."

"Casualties?" Tiberius's voice was clipped.

"Too many to count." Izzy swallowed hard. "The medbay's overflowing."

Her stomach churned, but she forced herself to remain focused. "What do they want?"

"Isn't it obvious?" Tiberius asked. "They want to plunder everything we have—our resources, our technology. That's what the Sventians do."

An explosion ripped through the far wall, showering them with debris. Tiberius shielded Simone with his body as chunks of metal rained down. "Get to the lab," he shouted over the din. "Lock yourselves in and activate the security protocols."

"I'm not leaving you." Simone's grip tightened on the pistol, her jaw set with determination.

Tiberius's eyes bored into hers, a tempest of emotions swirling in their depths. "This is my fight, Simone. I need you safe."

The thunderous boom of boots against the metal floor reverberated through the corridor. Her head whipped around, eyes widening at the sight of a towering figure striding toward them, flanked by a dozen heavily armed soldiers.

Tiberius tensed, his body coiled like a spring as he stepped in front of Simone. "Get behind me," he said, the laser pistol gripped tightly in his hand.

Vorn Drekar, the notorious leader of the Sventian Scourge, sneered as he entered the room. "If it isn't the great Tiberius Peña." His piercing blue eyes swept over Simone with undisguised disdain. "And a pretty little scientist."

Izzy inched closer to Simone, her fingers trembling as she clutched a datapad to her chest. "What do you want, Drekar?"

"Isn't it obvious?" Vorn's cybernetic claw flexed menacingly. "I want everything you've built here—your resources and your technology. This pathetic colony is mine for the taking. Putting Peña in charge invited me here, since he's the best." His tone was mocking.

"I've beaten you before on Sylko 7, and I'll do it again." Tiberius's jaw clenched, his muscles taut with barely restrained fury. "You'll get anything from our home over my dead body."

A cruel smile twisted Vorn's lips. "That can be arranged."

In a blur of movement, Tiberius launched himself at the Sventian leader, the two titans colliding with a bone-jarring impact. Laser blasts erupted around them as Vorn's soldiers opened fire, forcing Simone and Izzy to dive for cover.

Simone pressed herself against the wall, her heart pounding as Tiberius traded vicious blows with Vorn. The mercenary commander was a whirlwind of precision and power, his fists and feet finding their mark with devastating accuracy.

Yet Vorn matched him blow for blow, his cybernetic enhancements granting him unnatural strength and speed. He'd clearly been to the outer rims, where she'd heard rumors of experiments and researchers who didn't worry about things like ethics. His enhancements were crude but far too effective. A vicious backhand from his metal claw caught Tiberius across the face, drawing a crimson arc through the air.

Izzy cried out, her voice laced with anguish, but Simone remained transfixed, unable to tear her gaze away from the brutal spectacle unfolding before her.

Tiberius staggered, his lip split and blood trickling from a gash above his eye, but he refused to yield. With a feral snarl, he launched himself at Vorn once more, the two combatants grappling in a deadly dance of violence.

Simone's knuckles whitened as she gripped the laser pistol, her mind racing. She couldn't let Tiberius sacrifice himself for them. Not when they were so close to unlocking the secrets of the biocircuit interface, to changing the course of human evolution forever...and when she loved him with all her heart.

Her gaze darted around the command center, searching for anything that could turn the tide. They settled on a control panel, its buttons blinking ominously. Without hesitation, she scrambled toward it, ducking a stray laser blast that scorched the wall beside her.

"Simone, no." Izzy's voice was a strangled cry, but Simone paid it no heed.

Her fingers flew over the controls, inputting the emergency override sequence she had memorized for just such a contingency. With a final keystroke, the room plunged into darkness, the only illumination coming from the flickering emergency lights.

Vorn's soldiers faltered, their laser sights sweeping wildly through the gloom. Seizing the opportunity, she darted toward the melee, her heart in her throat.

Tiberius and Vorn were still locked in a brutal clinch, their bodies glistening with sweat and blood. Simone raised the pistol, her aim steady as she sighted down the barrel.

"Tiberius, get down." she shouted, her voice ringing with a conviction she didn't feel.

He didn't hesitate, dropping to one knee and exposing Vorn's back. Simone squeezed the trigger, the laser blast searing through the air and slamming into Vorn's upper back with a sickening hiss of scorched flesh, leaving a ragged two-inch hole that would have killed anyone not enhanced.

The Sventian leader bellowed in rage and pain, staggering backward as smoke curled from the charred wound. His gaze found Simone, burning with hatred and promised retribution. "You'll pay for that, bitch," he said harshly, clutching his ruined shoulder.

Tiberius surged to his feet, placing himself between Simone and Vorn once more. "Leave, Drekar," he said, his voice laced with menace, "Before I finish what she started."

For a long, tense moment, Vorn held Tiberius's gaze, his jaw clenched in a rictus of fury. Then, with a curt nod to his soldiers, he turned and stalked away, his boots ringing against the metal floor.

Simone sagged against the wall, her legs trembling as the adrenaline ebbed from her veins. Izzy rushed to her side, enveloping her in a fierce embrace. "You saved us," she whispered, her voice thick with emotion. "You saved all of us."

Simone could only nod mutely, her gaze fixed on Tiberius. He stood motionless, his chest heaving, blood streaking his face and matting his dark hair. Then, with agonizing slowness, he crumpled to the floor.

The medbay was a flurry of controlled chaos as Lancer and Hawk rushed Tiberius through the doors, his limp body cradled in their arms. Simone's heart raced, her mind reeling from the violence that had erupted mere moments ago.

"Over here." A medic waved them toward an empty biobed, her face grim. Lancer gently laid down Tiberius, and Simone gasped at the extent of his injuries. His face was a mask of blood and bruises, his left hand a mangled ruin of shredded flesh and splintered bone.

Izzy's hand found Simone's, gripping it tightly as the medics swarmed around Tiberius, their voices a litany of urgent commands and grim assessments.

"Multiple lacerations...severe blood loss..."

"Crushed femur, possible arterial damage..."

"Prepping for emergency surgery..."

Simone's gaze locked onto Tiberius's face, searching for any sign of consciousness, or any flicker of recognition in his half-lidded eyes, but his expression remained slack, his features devoid of the fierce determination that had burned within him mere moments ago.

A medic approached, her expression solemn. "Dr. Wiley, we need to stabilize the commander before we can proceed with surgery." She gestured to a nearby monitor, its display a jumble of flickering vitals and diagnostic readouts. "His injuries are...extensive. Even with our advanced technology, his chances of survival are slim."

Simone's breath caught in her throat, her vision blurring with unshed tears. She blinked them back, her jaw set with grim resolve. "No," she said, her voice trembling but laced with steel. "We're not losing him. Not after everything we've been through."

Izzy's fingers tightened around hers, a silent show of support.

Lancer stepped forward, his expression etched with concern. "Simone, the medics know what they're doing. You have to let them—"

"No." Simone cut him off, her eyes blazing with determination. "I won't accept those odds. Not when we're on the cusp of a breakthrough that could change everything."

Comprehension dawned on Izzy's face, her eyes widening. "The biocircuit interface..."

Simone nodded, her gaze never wavering from Tiberius's battered form. "It's our only chance to save him."

The medic shook her head, her brow furrowed with concern. "Dr. Wiley, that technology is still experimental. We have no way of knowing the consequences—"

"We don't have a choice." Simone's voice rang with conviction, silencing the medbay. "Tiberius is dying, and conventional medicine can't save him, but the biocircuit interface can."

She turned to Izzy, her eyes pleading. "Prep the lab. We'll need to move him there immediately."

Izzy hesitated for a heartbeat, then nodded. "On it." With a final squeeze of Simone's hand, she darted from the medbay, her footsteps echoing down the corridor.

Lancer stepped closer, his hazel eyes searching Simone's face. "Are you sure about this?" His voice was low and laced with concern. "Turning Tiberius into...into a cyborg? That's a hell of a decision to make for someone else."

Simone's gaze flickered to Tiberius's ruined hand, her throat tightening. "I don't have a choice," she whispered. "It's the only way to save his life." The thought of living without him was dismal and crushing, shrouding her in darkness. Maybe she was being selfish, but she'd save him no matter the cost, even if he hated her for it.

With a curt nod, Lancer turned to the medics. "You heard the lady. Let's get him prepped for transport."

As the medical team sprang into action, Simone allowed herself a moment of vulnerability, her mask of professionalism slipping. She reached out, brushing her fingers against Tiberius's bloodied cheek. "Hold on," she said, her voice thick with emotion. "I'm not letting you go that easily."

Chapter 6—Simone

SIMONE'S EYES NARROWED with determination as she hovered over Tiberius's still form. The lab hummed with the steady thrum of life-support systems, but she refused to relinquish hope. Not when she was so close to a breakthrough that could save him.

"Prep the neural interface," she said to the medical team, her voice calm. "We're proceeding with the biocircuit integration."

Murmurs of concern rippled through the room, but she paid them no heed. Her focus remained on the readings flickering across the monitors, analyzing Tiberius's vitals with clinical precision.

"Doctor, the risks—"

"I'm aware of the risks," she cut off the protest, "But we're out of conventional options. This is our only chance."

Silence descended as the team recognized the finality in her tone. They moved with efficiency, calibrating the intricate machinery and running final diagnostics under Izzy's direction. At the heart of the setup loomed the fusion reactor, a towering marvel of engineering that would provide the immense power required for the delicate procedure.

As the preparations continued around her, her hands moved with practiced ease, making the final adjustments to the neural interface. This was the crux of the operation, the delicate link that would allow Tiberius's biological neurons to seamlessly integrate with the cybernetic enhancements they had installed to heal him after stabilizing the link.

"Initiating power transfer from the fusion reactor," said one of the medics.

The room seemed to hold its collective breath as the machinery whirred to life, energy crackling through the intricate web of circuits and conduits. Simone felt the familiar thrill of scientific discovery coursing through her veins, mingling with the undercurrent of trepidation that accompanied any untested procedure.

She couldn't falter when Tiberius's life hung in the balance. "Neural interface online and syncing," she said, her fingers moving across the control panel quickly. "Commencing integration sequence."

The air thrummed with energy as the biocircuit interface initiated its delicate work, weaving synthetic pathways into Tiberius's neural network. Simone watched with bated breath, her brilliant mind processing every fluctuation and nuance of data that streamed across the monitors.

Time seemed to slow as the intricate process unfolded, each second stretching into an eternity. Her world narrowed to the rhythmic beeps of the life-support systems and the subtle shifts in Tiberius's vital signs.

Then, without warning, a piercing alarm shattered the tense silence.

"Synaptic rejection," cried one of the medics, her voice laced with urgency. "The interface is destabilizing."

Simone's chest constricted as she fought to maintain control. This was the critical juncture, the moment where Tiberius's body would either accept or reject the cybernetic integration. "Increasing neural dampeners," she called out, adjusting the controls. "Modulating synaptic pathways to compensate."

The room held its collective breath as the machinery whirred and hummed, the fusion reactor thrumming with power as it fed the ravenous demands of the biocircuit interface. She grimaced, her mind a whirlwind of calculations and adjustments as she guided the process through the treacherous waters of rejection.

Seconds ticked by, each one an eternity unto itself, until finally, the alarms fell silent. The monitors flickered, displaying a steady stream of data that brought a relieved smile to Simone's lips.

"Integration successful," she said with wonder. "The biocircuit interface is stable."

A collective sigh of relief swept through the room, but Simone barely registered it. Her gaze was fixed on Tiberius, taking in the subtle changes that had already begun to manifest. His body, once ravaged by the Sventian blast, now hummed with newfound vitality, the cybernetic enhancements already working to repair the damage.

As she watched, his eyes flickered open, those warm brown depths locking onto hers with an intensity that stole her breath. They had crossed a threshold, venturing into uncharted territory, where the boundaries between human and machine blurred. She hoped he wouldn't hate her for this.

For a long moment, silence reigned, the steady beeps of the monitors the only sound in the sterile lab. She searched his face, analyzing every minute shift in his expression and every subtle twitch of muscle, for any sign of rejection or distress.

Tiberius's brow furrowed slightly, and he opened his mouth as if to speak, but no words came forth. Instead, his gaze drifted downward, taking in the intricate web of circuitry that now wove through his flesh, the gleaming conduits pulsing with blue energy from the thrum of the fusion reactor's power.

Simone held her breath as she awaited his reaction. Would he recoil in horror at what she had done? Would he curse her for violating the sanctity of his body, for blurring the lines between human and machine?

A flicker of emotion passed across his features—confusion, perhaps, or a hint of anxiety, but then, to her profound relief, his expression softened, and a smile tugged at the corners of his mouth. "You did it, you crazy, brilliant woman."

Simone exhaled a shaky breath, her shoulders sagging as the tension drained from her body. "How do you feel?" she asked.

He flexed his fingers, his movements fluid and precise, belying the intricate cybernetic enhancements that now coursed through his veins and into the cybernetic arm and hand. His had been inoperable, so they'd amputated it and replaced it with the sleek new tech. "Different," he said after a moment's pause, "But not... unpleasant."

A soft chuckle escaped Simone's lips, tinged with a hint of giddy relief. "That's quite the understatement, Commander."

His gaze met hers once more, and she saw a depth of understanding as he grasped what she'd done. They had ventured into uncharted territory, defying the boundaries of what it meant to be human, and emerged on the other side, forever changed. She'd volunteered him for that, but he didn't seem upset.

"Tell me everything. I want to know it all."

Simone nodded. Where to begin? The biocircuit interface was a marvel of engineering, a delicate fusion of organic and synthetic components that pushed the limits of what was possible.

Drawing a steadying breath, she launched into an explanation, her words tumbling forth in a torrent of scientific jargon and technical details. She spoke of the neural interface and the intricate pathways that allowed Tiberius's biological neurons to seamlessly integrate with the cybernetic enhancements. She described the bio-compatible materials, designed to minimize rejection and encourage the growth of natural tissues around the implants.

As she delved deeper into the intricacies of the technology, she was growing more animated, her hands gesturing emphatically as she painted a vivid picture of the self-healing circuits and adaptive learning algorithms that would allow Tiberius's new abilities to evolve and adapt over time.

Throughout her impassioned monologue, he listened closely, his expression hard to read. Occasionally, he would interject with a question, probing deeper into the science behind the procedure, and Simone would eagerly expound, her brilliant mind reveling in the opportunity to share her knowledge.

Time seemed to blur as they lost themselves in the intricacies of the technology. It was only when a discreet cough from one of the medical technicians broke the spell that Simone realized how long she had been speaking. A flush crept up her neck, and she ducked her head sheepishly, suddenly self-conscious of her exuberance.

Tiberius merely chuckled, his eyes crinkling at the corners with amusement. "Forgive me, Doctor," he said, his tone rich with affection. "I seem to have unleashed a torrent of scientific passion."

Simone felt her cheeks grow warmer, but she returned his smile. "Apologies, Tiberius. I got a bit carried away."

A comfortable silence settled between them. Simone was studying Tiberius anew, marveling at the subtle changes that had already begun to manifest. His movements, always fluid and graceful, now carried a hint of enhanced precision, each gesture infused with a newfound economy of motion. His eyes seemed sharper, more focused, as if he could perceive the world around him with heightened clarity.

And yet, beneath these outward transformations, Simone could still see the essence of the man she had come to know and admire—the courage, the loyalty, and quiet strength that had drawn her to him from the moment they first met.

SIMONE'S HEART FLUTTERED when she was finally alone with Tiberius in the secluded alcove of the medbay, having moved him back there for monitoring after the procedure. The hum of machinery faded into the background, muffled by the electronic privacy screens that cordoned off their intimate space.

She take in the sight of him, her gaze roving over the intricate web of circuitry that now intertwined with his flesh. The biocircuit interface pulsed with a faint, green glow as the fusion reactor's power coursed through his veins.

Tiberius met her scrutiny with a steady gaze, his warm brown eyes holding a depth of emotion that stole her breath. For a long moment, they simply regarded each other in silence.

At last, he broke the stillness. "You're troubled." It wasn't a question, but a statement of fact, spoken with quiet certainty.

Simone swallowed hard, suddenly aware of the rapid staccato of her heartbeat. "I..." She faltered, struggling to find the words to articulate the maelstrom of emotions swirling within her. "I never imagined it would come to this. That you'd be the first..." Guilt hit her as she trailed off.

Tiberius arched a brow, his expression inscrutable. "You had doubts about the procedure?"

Simone shook her head vehemently. "No, never. The science was sound, the calculations precise. I had every confidence in the technology." She paused, worrying her lower lip between her teeth. "But to see it manifested in you, to witness the transformation firsthand..."

Her voice trailed off, and she was reaching out, her fingers tracing the intricate patterns etched into his skin. The circuitry hummed beneath her touch, thrumming with a subtle vibration that spoke of immense power contained within.

He held himself perfectly still, allowing her exploration, his gaze never wavering from her face. "You're afraid," he said, his tone devoid of judgment. "Afraid of what I've become."

Simone recoiled as if struck, her hand falling away from his flesh. "No." The vehemence in her voice surprised even her. "Never that, Tiberius. I could never fear you."

A ghost of a smile tugged at the corners of his mouth, and he reached out, brushing a stray lock of hair from her face. The gesture was achingly tender, a stark contrast to the enhanced strength and precision she knew now coursed through his veins.

"Then what troubles you, my love?"

She drew a shuddering breath, her mind whirling as she sought to put her tumultuous emotions into words. "I fear..." She paused, her gaze locking onto his. "I fear what this will cost you."

Tiberius's brow furrowed, confusion flickering across his features. "Cost me? Simone, you've given me a gift beyond measure. A chance to not only survive but to become something more, something greater than I ever imagined, and to continue to be with you instead of dying."

Simone shook her head, her heart aching at his words. "But at what price, Tiberius? You've sacrificed a part of your humanity, your very essence, to become this fusion of flesh and machine."

Her voice wavered, and she was gripping his hand, her fingers entwining with his as if seeking an anchor in the storm of her doubts. "I made that choice for you, without your consent. I violated the sanctity of your body, blurred the lines between human and machine, all in the name of saving your life and not having to live without you."

Tiberius regarded her for a long moment, his expression unreadable. Then, with a gentleness that belied his newfound strength, he lifted her hand to his lips, pressing a light kiss to her knuckles. "You did what you had to do, Simone," he said, his voice rich with emotion. "You saved me, not just from death, but from the oblivion that awaited beyond, and in doing so, you've given me a gift more precious than you can imagine."

Simone's breath caught in her throat as he drew her closer, his arms enfolding her in a tender embrace. She could feel the thrum of the fusion reactor against her cheek, a steady pulse that spoke of life.

"This is not a sacrifice, but a transformation. A chance to become something greater, something more than the sum of our parts." He drew back slightly, his gaze boring into hers with an intensity that stole her breath away. "Do you not see, Simone? You've given me the opportunity to truly protect this colony, to safeguard the future we're building here. With these enhancements, I'm more than just a soldier or a mercenary. I'm a guardian."

Simone's doubts wavered, her fears ebbing in the face of his confidence and conviction. She searched his eyes, seeking any hint of regret or uncertainty but found only certainty. "You're not... afraid?" she asked, her voice barely above a whisper. "Of what you've become, of the changes you've undergone?"

Tiberius chuckled. "Afraid?" he echoed, his lips curving into a wry smile. "Simone, my love, I'm excited, not afraid. I get to be with you, and I can protect everything we have here, because Vorn will return." His expression darkened for a moment with those words.

Then he cupped her face, his touch achingly gentle yet infused with a newfound precision that spoke of his enhanced abilities. "I'm not afraid, Simone. I'm in awe of my new abilities and your ability to make this possible."

Her doubts and fears dissipated like mist. She leaned into his touch, reveling in the solidity of his embrace, and the reassuring thrum of the fusion reactor that now beat in tandem with her own heart.

"I'm so relieved. I thought I might save you only to lose you because you couldn't forgive me," she whispered.

"There's nothing to forgive." He kissed her deeply, making the monitor tracking his heartrate beep.

That made her laugh, and she held him for a long moment, enjoying his presence and happy he was still with her. Most importantly, he still loved her. He hadn't said those words yet, and neither had she, but she was certain that's what this overwhelming emotion was that burned between them.

Chapter 7—Tiberius

THE FIRST RAYS OF DAWN filtered through the reinforced windows of the medbay. Tiberius stirred, his newly enhanced senses attuned to the subtlest changes in his environment. He took a deep breath, his synthetic right lung processing the recycled air with remarkable efficiency. He could feel a difference in performance between the right and left, which was his original human-issue.

Beside him, Simone slept fitfully in a chair, her head resting on the edge of his bed. He'd tried to coax her to lie down with him, but she'd insisted he needed to be monitored and not overly stimulated for a while. Tiberius studied her features, etched with concern even in slumber. She had refused to leave his side throughout the arduous procedure and since he woke up afterward.

Flexing his fingers, he marveled at the fluidity of the cybernetic enhancements fused with his flesh. The biocircuit interface thrummed with energy, its neural pathways seamlessly integrated into his nervous system. The power coursed through his body, a constant hum just beneath his consciousness that was soothing rather than irritating.

Simone shifted, her eyes fluttering open. "Tiberius?" She straightened, blinking away the remnants of sleep. "How are you feeling?"

"Incredible." His voice resonated with a subtle vibration, a byproduct of the enhancements. "Just like last night. I'm ready to get up."

Relief washed over her features as she reached for his hand, her fingers tracing the intricate circuitry patterns etched into his skin. "We have so much to explore. Your potential is limitless now."

Tiberius nodded, his mind already processing the myriad possibilities. Yet a part of him felt unmoored and adrift in this new reality. He had been a soldier, a protector—but what was he now? He realized he'd asked that aloud when she answered him.

Simone leaned closer. "I know this is a profound change, but you're still you, Tiberius. Your core...your heart...*you*...remains unaltered."

He held her gaze. "I know that, but I'm still worried. I guess I will be until I test all my limits."

She smiled, taking his hand. "If you feel up to it, we can start testing now."

OVER THE NEXT WEEK, Tiberius immersed himself in the process of understanding his new capabilities. Each day brought fresh discoveries and challenges, but Simone's presence helped ground him.

In the training room, he learned to harness his enhanced strength and speed. Simone monitored the readouts, adjusting the parameters to push his limits. "Concentrate on the neural pathways. Feel the energy flow and let it guide your movements."

Tiberius closed his eyes, his mind syncing with the biocircuit interface. He could sense every circuit pulsing with power. With a deep exhalation, he unleashed a flurry of strikes, his fists and feet a blur of motion. The training drones struggled to keep up, their defensive algorithms overwhelmed by his newfound agility.

Simone's delighted laughter rang out. "Incredible. You're adapting faster than I anticipated."

Tiberius shared her enthusiasm, a rare grin spreading across his features. The experience and how invincible he felt were amazing.

Later that day, Simone guided him through cognitive exercises, testing the limits of his parallel processing capabilities. "Multitask these simulations while we discuss the fusion reactor schematics."

Tiberius nodded, his mind effortlessly dividing its focus. He absorbed the complex data streams while conversing with Simone, his thoughts flowing with crystalline clarity.

"Remarkable," she said, her eyes alight with wonder. "You're processing information at a rate I've never witnessed before."

Tiberius felt a swell of pride, tempered by a lingering unease. This newfound power was intoxicating, but it also felt alien, a departure from the man he once was.

Late one night, as they pored over the latest test results, Simone sensed his disquiet. "What troubles you, Tiberius?"

He hesitated, grappling with the words. "I feel...disconnected from my former self. As if the man I was is slipping away, replaced by this enhanced being."

Simone's expression softened with understanding. "You're still that man. These enhancements are tools, just extensions of your true self. They don't define you."

Her words were comforting. As their gazes locked, he saw her love for him shining there and knew, no matter how drastically his physical form had changed, his essence remained intact.

THE COLONY BUSTLED with activity as the mercs and civilians worked tirelessly to fortify their defenses after the unexpected previous invasion. Tiberius strode through the corridors, his cybernetic enhancements thrumming with power, his gaze sweeping over the flurry of preparations. Everything came so much easier now that he could do a hundred tasks at once and give each the necessary attention.

In the armory, Lance supervised the distribution of munitions, his brow furrowed in concentration. As Tiberius approached, his friend's expression brightened. "Commander. It's good to have you back on duty."

Tiberius nodded, his synthetic muscles rippling beneath his combat gear. "Status report."

"Perimeter defenses are at eighty percent and rising. We've reinforced the outer walls and set up a network of automated turrets." Lance's hazel eyes gleamed with determination. "If those Sventian bastards show their faces again, we'll be ready."

A slight smirk tugged at Tiberius's lips. "Excellent work, Major." He clasped Lance's shoulder, the biocircuit interface pulsing with energy at the contact. "I'll need you to oversee the final preparations. I have a meeting with Sim...Dr. Wiley."

Lance's expression shifted, awe and envy flickering across his features. "About your...enhancements?"

Tiberius arched an eyebrow, his heightened senses detecting the subtle shift in his friend's demeanor. "Among other things."

"I've been thinking..." Lance hesitated, his gaze dropping momentarily before locking with Tiberius's. "If the opportunity arises, I want to undergo the procedure too."

A weighted silence stretched between them, charged with unspoken implications. Finally, Tiberius inclined his head. "We'll discuss it later. For now, focus on securing the colony."

With a curt nod, Lance turned back to the armory, barking orders to the mercs as they loaded crates of ammunition onto hovercarts.

Tiberius made his way to the command center, his footfalls silent on the polished floors. As he entered, he caught Simone's eye, her gaze lingering on the intricate circuitry patterns that now adorned his skin.

"Tiberius," she said, her voice warm yet laced with a hint of professionalism. "I trust Dr. Valeria has cleared you for active duty?"

"She has." He stepped closer, his enhanced senses attuned to the subtle floral notes of her shampoo. "Though I suspect her medical expertise will be unnecessary, given my new...resilience."

A faint smile curved Simone's lips. "Even so, I'd prefer to err on the side of caution. Your integration was a success, but there's still so much to learn."

Tiberius nodded, his gaze holding hers. "Then I'm fortunate to have such a brilliant teacher."

A slight flush crept into Simone's cheeks, but before she could respond, Izzy's voice cut through the command center. "Oi, lovebirds. We've got work to do."

Simone shot Izzy a playful glare, but her expression quickly sobered as she turned back to Tiberius. "Let's get to it, then."

As they pored over the schematics and defensive strategies, Tiberius was acutely aware of Simone's presence. The way she leaned closer to point out a detail, the subtle scent of her perfume, and the warmth of her breath all seemed amplified by his enhanced senses.

Hours later, as twilight descended over the colony, he was in the courtyard, overseeing the final touches on the perimeter defenses. A familiar figure approached, and he turned to find Lance striding toward him. "Everything's in place, Commander. We're as ready as we'll ever be."

Tiberius nodded, his synthetic muscles coiling with anticipation. "Good. The Sventian Scourge will face formidable resistance this time."

Lance's gaze flickered over Tiberius's cybernetic enhancements, a hint of longing in his eyes. "I meant what I said earlier about undergoing the procedure."

Tiberius studied his friend, weighing his request. "It's a significant transformation, Lance. Are you prepared for the consequences?"

"I am." Lance's jaw tightened with resolve. "If it means protecting the colony and protecting our people, I'll do whatever it takes."

A heavy silence stretched between them, the weight of Lance's words hanging in the air. Finally, Tiberius inclined his head. "Very well. We'll discuss it with Simone."

Lance's shoulders sagged with relief, a grateful smile tugging at his lips. "Thank you, Commander. I won't let you down."

As Lance turned to rejoin the mercs, Tiberius felt a presence behind him. He pivoted, his enhanced reflexes kicking in, only to find Simone approaching.

"I overheard Lance's request."

Tiberius arched an eyebrow, his synthetic skin rippling with the subtle movement. "And your thoughts?"

Simone's expression sobered. "While I'm thrilled at the prospect of enhancing more individuals, I think it's best if we proceed cautiously. Let your integration serve as a test case for now."

Before Tiberius could respond, Simone stepped closer, grazing his arm in a light caress. "We've come so far, but there's still much to learn."

Her touch sent a jolt of electricity through Tiberius's circuits, his enhanced senses heightening the intimacy of the moment. He opened his mouth to reply, but the words caught in his throat as Simone's hand trailed lower, her fingers brushing against the small of his back.

A low, rumbling chuckle escaped her lips. "Easy there, big guy. We have work to do."

With a playful swat to his backside, Simone turned and strode away, leaving Tiberius equal parts exhilarated and bewildered by her bold gesture.

As he watched her retreating form, a smile tugged at his lips. The Sventian Scourge would face more than just fortified defenses if they were foolish enough to return. hey would confront a united front.

HE WOKE WITH A START, reaching for his laser pistol out of habit. Tiberius blinked to see Simone slipping into his bed. "Is everything okay? Are the Sventian Scourge back to attack us again?"

She shook her head, shyly slipping the strap of her nightgown off her shoulder in an enticing fashion. "I've missed you. Doc cleared you for duty, so I assume your little soldier is in top form too?" She grinned even as she blushed.

Tiberius smiled, realizing what she wanted. "Oh, yes, I'm ready for action, Doc."

Simone giggled as she crawled into bed, her naked body pressing against his. "Good, because I'm in the mood for some rough and dirty sex. Can you handle that, soldier?"

He growled as he rolled her onto her back, pinning her wrists above her head. She winced, and he realized he'd overgripped with his new cybernetic hand. "Sorry, I'm not used to my new strength. Let me make it up to you."

"Yes, please," she whispered, her eyes wide with anticipation.

He kissed her deeply, letting go of her wrists so he could explore her body with his hands. To his surprise, the only difference between his bionic hand and his own hand was he could feel her skin even better. She drew in her breath, trembling when he lightly tweaked her nipple with his cybernetic fingers. She shivered, and he asked, "Cold?"

She shrugged. "The bare metal is a little cold, but Izzy's working on synthetic skin. It won't always be possible to use it to cover enhancements, but it should work on a spot like your hand."

"That would be nice," he said, kissing her again before adding, "But I'm not sure I want to hide my hand. I'm proud of my new abilities. I can do things I never dreamed of before. I'm stronger, faster, and I have a built-in weapon. I'm a cyborg, and I'm damn proud of it." Despite his words, he had a niggle of doubt. Would she be able to accept the changes in him? Was she contrasting his current body with the one he'd had the last time they made love?

She must have sensed his doubt, because she reached down, stroking his cock, which was already hard and throbbing. "You're still the same man, and I'm not afraid of the changes. I know you'll never hurt me, and I trust you. I'm just glad I didn't lose you. I don't care if you're a cyborg, a robot, or a human. You're alive, and that's all that matters. Now, stop talking and fuck me, Tiberius."

He laughed as he grasped her wrists again. "You mentioned hard and rough?"

She moaned and wiggled against him, lightly testing his grip. "Yes, please."

He kissed her, then flipped her onto her stomach, pulling her up to her knees. He slapped her ass, and she yelped. "Harder."

He spanked her again, and she groaned. "More."

He grinned as he positioned his mouth near her ear. "I'm going to fuck you hard and fast, and I'm not going to let go of your wrists. If you need me to stop, say 'lunar.' Do you understand?"

She nodded, her breathing heavy with excitement. "Yes, I understand. Fuck me, Tiberius. Fuck me hard."

He pressed the head of his cock against her wet opening, teasing her for a moment before thrusting deeply inside her. She cried out, her pussy clenching around him as he filled her. "Oh, god."

"Did you change your mind?" he asked near her ear again.

"No, keep going. Please, don't stop."

He thrust into her, setting a punishing pace. She was so wet and tight, and her moans and whimpers only fueled his desire. He gripped her wrists tightly, holding her in place as he fucked her. She bucked against him, matching his rhythm and begging for more.

"Please, harder. I need to feel all of you. I was so close to losing you..." Her voice trailed off, but it was thick with emotion.

He should probably stop to make sure she was in the right frame of mind, but then she clenched her inner muscles around him, and he groaned. His hips snapped forward, and he drove into her with renewed vigor. She gasped and shuddered, her body tensing as her orgasm hit. "Yes, yes, yes." Her pussy clamped down on him like a vice.

He gritted his teeth, fighting back his own release as her body trembled with pleasure. She was so beautiful, and he was so lucky to have her. His heart swelled with love for her, and he vowed to never take her for granted.

"I love you, Simone," he whispered, kissing her neck.

She turned her head to look at him, her eyes shining with unshed tears. "I love you too, Tiberius, but you still haven't come, and I could probably come again..." She tilted her head flirtatiously while squeezing around his cock again.

He chuckled, shaking his head. "You're insatiable, woman."

She smiled, her eyes dancing with mischief. "Only for you, my love. Now, give me what I want, and I'll give you what you want."

"As you wish, my lady." He pulled her ass up and entered her from behind again. She moaned, arching her back and pushing her ass against him. He thrust into her, gripping her hips and pulling her to him. She was so wet and tight, and she felt amazing.

"I'm never going to get enough of you, my love. I'm going to fuck you every day for the rest of our lives," he said, thrusting into her.

She whimpered, her body trembling as another orgasm washed over her. "Promise?"

He leaned down, nibbling her earlobe. "I promise."

He continued to thrust into her, bringing them both to the brink of ecstasy before dragging the head of his cock against her clit as he withdrew and plunged into her again, burying himself balls-deep. They came together, their bodies shuddering with pleasure as they collapsed in a heap of sweaty limbs.

He kissed the top of her head, holding her close. "I'm the luckiest man in the world to have you in my life."

She snuggled closer, sighing contentedly. "And I'm the luckiest woman in the world to have you in mine. I love you, Tiberius."

"I love you too, Simone. I always will."

They basked in the afterglow of their lovemaking. The sound of the rain pattering against the window filled the room, and the scent of sex permeated the air. It was the perfect moment, and he never wanted it to end.

Chapter 8—Simone

SIMONE STRODE ALONGSIDE Tiberius down the pristine corridor, the soft hum of machinery surrounding them. Her ponytail swayed with each purposeful step, and the crisp scent of disinfectant mingled with the earthy notes of potted plants lining the hall.

"Brick sounded urgent on the comm," said Tiberius, his deep voice reverberating. "I'm not sure what this is about."

Simone nodded, her brow furrowing slightly. "I hope it's nothing too serious." The possibility of another Sventian attack was never far from her mind, and her stomach clenched at the idea.

They turned a corner, and Tiberius palmed open a door, revealing a spacious office. Brick, one of the Iron Wolves mercenaries, stood by the window, his muscular frame silhouetted against the vibrant alien sky.

"You wanted to see me?" asked Tiberius, his tone clipped.

Brick pivoted, his expression grave. "We've got a situation, Commander." His gaze flickered to Simone. "Might be best if the doc hears this too."

Tiberius gestured for him to continue, his jaw tightening imperceptibly.

"Scout team picked up chatter about a potential raid," said Brick, his words measured. "Word is, the Sventian Scourge is coming back for more. They want the tech for themselves, but Vorn wants the doc dead for shooting him."

A heavy silence hung in the air as Simone processed the information. The Sventian Scourge, a ruthless band of space pirates, were coming back. Even worse, she was personally marked for death after shooting their leader.

"When?" Tiberius's single word carried a weight that made the hairs on Simone's nape prickle.

"Intercepted transmissions suggest they'll strike within the next cycle," said Brick grimly. "We need to finish fortifying our defenses, and fast."

Tiberius nodded, his expression hardening. "Gather the team. We'll strategize and implement countermeasures immediately and verify all our previous plans are finished." His gaze met Simone's, a silent question in his eyes.

She understood his unspoken query. "The biocircuit integration could give us an edge," she said, her mind already whirring with possibilities. "If we can enhance the remaining Iron Wolves, their reaction times and combat capabilities would increase exponentially."

Tiberius's features softened ever so slightly, a glimmer of pride flickering in his eyes. "You're certain the procedure is ready for widespread implementation?"

"I'm as sure as I can be with you as our only data point." She shrugged. "We've ironed out the kinks, and the fusion reactor is stable. With your team's skills combined with cybernetic enhancements, we'll be an unstoppable force, but it should be voluntary."

Brick shifted, his expression a mix of curiosity and alarm. "You want to turn us into cyborgs, doc?"

Simone met his gaze steadily. "Not cyborgs, per se. More like...augmented humans. The biocircuit interface integrates seamlessly with your biological systems, enhancing your natural abilities without compromising your humanity."

Tiberius nodded, his jaw set with determination. "Brick, assemble the team in the briefing room. We'll go over the details and address any concerns."

As Brick departed, Tiberius turned to Simone, his eyes burning with an intensity that sent a frisson of electricity through her veins. "You ready for this?"

She reached out, her fingers brushing his arm, the contact sending a jolt of energy through her circuits. "Yes." Her voice was laden with conviction and something deeper, more primal.

Tiberius held her gaze for a heartbeat longer before giving a curt nod. "Then let's get to work. The Sventian Scourge won't know what hit them." Side by side, they strode from the office, their steps in sync.

THE BRIEFING ROOM HUMMED with a taut energy as Simone addressed the assembled Iron Wolves. Tiberius stood at her side, his presence a reassuring bulwark against the weight of the situation.

"I know this is a lot to take in," she said, her voice carrying calm authority she deliberately infused, "But the biocircuit integration is our best chance against the Sventian threat."

Izzy stepped forward, a holographic display flickering to life beside her. "The procedure involves integrating an advanced neural interface directly into your cerebral cortex." Detailed schematics rotated in the air, illustrating the intricate technology. "This will allow seamless communication between your biological neurons and the cybernetic enhancements."

A low murmur rippled through the mercenaries, their expressions ranging from curiosity to outright skepticism. Hawk, the team's sharp-eyed sniper, raised a slender hand. "And these...enhancements? What exactly are we talking about?"

Simone's lips curved into a faint smile. "Enhanced cognitive processing speeds, augmented senses, and increased strength and reaction times. With the fusion reactor powering the neural interface, you'll be operating at peak human capacity...and beyond."

Lancer, the team's resident tech expert, leaned forward, his eyes alight with interest. "Essentially, we become...cyborgs?"

"Not quite," said Tiberius, his deep voice commanding attention. "You'll retain your humanity, your free will. The enhancements will amplify your existing abilities without compromising who you are."

Doc, the team's medic, frowned. "And the risks? We're talking about rewriting our neural pathways here."

Izzy's fingers tapped across the holographic controls, pulling up a new set of schematics. "The biocircuit materials are bio-compatible, designed to integrate seamlessly with your biological systems. We've run countless simulations, and the procedure is as safe as we can make it."

Silence hung heavy in the room as the Iron Wolves digested the information. Finally, Brick said, "If it means keeping this colony safe, I'm in."

One by one, the others nodded their assent, their expressions hardening. All except Hawk, who remained still, her brow wrinkled. She exhaled slowly, her shoulders rising and falling. "I...need some time to think about this."

Simone offered her a reassuring smile. "Of course. This is a big decision, and we want you all to be certain." Her gaze swept over the assembled team. "Get some rest. We'll begin the procedures at 0600 tomorrow on anyone who volunteers. This isn't compulsory."

THE MEDBAY THRUMMED with a focused energy as Simone and Izzy made the final preparations, converting one of the rooms to a makeshift lab to make the process go faster and smoother, since the lab wasn't really equipped for conversions. They'd made it work with Tiberius due to necessity, but she wanted it to be easier this time with the number of conversions ahead of them. Banks of monitors cast a cool, blue glow over the sterile space, and the air carried the faint tang of disinfectant.

"Neural interface is online and synced," said Izzy, fingers moving over the holographic controls. "Fusion reactor is primed and ready for power transfer."

Simone nodded, her gaze sweeping over the assembled Iron Wolves. Brick, Lancer, and Doc lay on the bio-beds, their expressions stoic but all revealing some level of anxiety. Tiberius stood vigil, his presence a reassuring constant. Hawk had opted out, at least thus far.

"Initiating neural integration sequence," said Simone, voice ringing with calm authority.

A series of soft whirs and clicks filled the air as the intricate machinery hummed to life. Simone watched, her heart accelerating as the neural interfaces extended hairline tendrils, delicately breaching the mercenaries' skulls and interfacing with their cerebral cortices.

Brick tensed, his massive frame going rigid for a heartbeat before relaxing. "Whoa…" His voice held a note of wonder. "It's like…my mind just expanded."

Lance's eyes widened, his gaze darting around the room with newfound clarity. "I can process everything so quickly. It's…incredible."

Doc remained silent, his expression one of intense focus as the integration sequence reached its crescendo.

"Power transfer commencing," said Izzy. "Fusion reactor output at fifteen percent and rising."

A low thrum filled the air, the vibrations resonating in Simone's bones as the reactor poured its energy into the neural interfaces. Readouts flickered across the monitors, data streaming in a dizzying cascade of numbers and waveforms.

Simone held her breath, every fiber of her being focused on the intricate dance of technology and biology unfolding before her. This was the moment, the culmination of years of research and countless sleepless nights.

"Reactor output at fifty percent," called out Izzy, her voice taut with concentration. "Biocircuit integration holding steady."

Tiberius moved closer, his gaze locked on the monitors and his expression inscrutable. Simone was drawn to him, his presence anchoring her amidst the maelstrom of data and energy.

"Eighty percent and rising," said Izzy.

Simone's fingers tightened around the railing, her knuckles whitening with the strain. The thrum built to a crescendo, the air itself seeming to vibrate with the sheer power coursing through the biocircuit interfaces. Her heart paused for a full beat as her every sense attuned to the events unfolding.

In a blinding surge of energy, the fusion reactor reached its peak output, flooding the neural interfaces with its boundless power. For a breathless moment, the world seemed to hold its breath. Tiberius stumbled slightly, clearly getting a full jolt of the power. It had been hovering around eighty percent for him until now, after Izzy made some refinements during their preparations.

With a series of soft chimes, the monitors practically spat out data, displaying a dizzying array that spoke of seamless integration and optimal functionality.

"It worked..." Izzy's voice was a reverent whisper, her eyes wide with awe. "They're online and at max power."

Simone exhaled a shuddering breath, sagging with relief and exhilaration. She turned to Tiberius, her eyes shining with unshed tears of joy and triumph.

He grinned at her. "It's a helluva a rush, love."

She laughed at that as the Iron Wolves stirred, their eyes flickering open with clarity and purpose. Simone allowed herself a moment to bask in the achievement. They had taken the first step into a bold, new frontier, and the path ahead promised untold wonders and challenges, but for now, they had made history.

THE PROCEDURE HAD GONE flawlessly for Brick, Lancer, and Doc, but as Simone turned her attention to Hawk, who'd arrived moments before with the last-minute decision to upgrade, a sense of unease rippled through her. The lithe sniper lay motionless on the bio-bed, her features etched with a tension that belied the serene environment of the med-bay.

Simone moved closer, her steps quiet on the sterile floor. "Hawk?" She kept her voice low, mindful of the other mercenaries, who were still acclimating to their new abilities. "Are you ready?"

Hawk's gray eyes flicked open, revealing apprehension, uncertainty, and a fleeting glimpse of vulnerability rarely seen in the unflappable warrior. With a slow exhalation, Hawk gave a curt nod. "Do it."

Simone felt Tiberius move to her side, his presence reassuring. She drew strength from his proximity, allowing it to steady her as she initiated the neural integration sequence.

The air hummed with energy as the delicate tendrils extended, breaching Hawk's skull with surgical precision. Simone watched enthralled, certain she'd never get tired of watching this process. Her breath caught in her throat as the neural interface established its connection, weaving itself into the intricate tapestry of Hawk's mind.

For a moment, all was still, the only sound the soft beeping of the monitors. Then, Hawk's body went rigid, her back arching as a strangled gasp tore from her lips.

"Hawk?" Tiberius's voice was a low rumble of concern as he moved closer.

Hawk's eyes flew open, wide and wild, her gaze darting around the room with a feral intensity. Her chest heaved, each breath coming in ragged gasps as her fingers clenched the edges of the bio-bed.

"Easy, soldier," said Tiberius, his tone carrying a gentle authority. "You're safe. Just breathe."

Hawk seemed not to hear him, trembling as a low, keening whine escaped her lips. Simone's chest constricted as she recognized the signs of a panic attack taking hold. "Izzy, abort the procedure," she said with urgency.

Izzy's fingers flew over the controls, but before she could initiate the abort sequence, Hawk's body went rigid once more. A guttural cry tore from her lips, raw and primal, as the neural interface completed its integration.

The monitors flickered to life, streaming data across the displays in a dizzying cascade of numbers and waveforms. Simone took a deep breath as she watched the readouts, her mind struggling to process what she was seeing.

"Simone..." Izzy's voice was hushed, tinged with awe and trepidation. "Her neural integration is off the charts. I've never seen anything like this."

"I'm not surprised. She's only the fifth person..." She trailed off, moving closer to the soldier still on the biobed.

Hawk's body thrashed, her muscles straining against invisible bonds as a low, guttural growl rumbled in her throat. Tiberius moved closer, looking frightened, but Simone held up a hand, halting him in his tracks.

"Wait..." She kept her voice low, her eyes locked on the wildly fluctuating readouts. "Something's happening, and we might kill her if we disrupt the process."

For a moment, he seemed poised to separate Hawk from the equipment anyway, but then he took a step back. The world seemed to hold its breath as, with a final, bone-rattling shudder, Hawk's body went still.

Silence descended, heavy and oppressive, as Simone watched the monitors with bated breath. Hawk wasn't dead, but her current state was ambiguous. Slowly, agonizingly, the readouts began to stabilize, the wild fluctuations evening out into a steady, rhythmic pulse.

Finally, her eyes flickered open, and Simone was caught in a gaze that seemed to pierce straight through to her soul. There was a razor-sharp focus that sent a shiver racing down her spine. It felt like Hawk could see her thoughts as she was thinking them.

"Hawk?" Tiberius's voice was laced with cautious concern.

For a heartbeat, she remained motionless, her eyes locked on Simone's. Then, with a slow, measured exhalation, she inclined her head in a subtle nod. "I'm...operational," she said, sounding the same as ever.

A tremor of relief coursed through Simone, tempered by a lingering sense of unease. She had witnessed something profound that defied her understanding of the biocircuit integration process.

As Hawk rose from the bio-bed, her movements fluid and graceful, Simone couldn't wait to see how the sniper performed on the integration tests. She had a feeling Hawk had acclimated and bonded with the biocircuits on a level far deeper than any of her comrades, even Tiberius. It was promising for the future, but she wanted to know Hawk's limits first.

Chapter 9—Simone

HAWK'S TESTING HAD proven she'd had a unique experience. She was even faster and processed more quickly than any of the other four. The challenge before them was to figure out how Hawk had adapted so well and replicate it to make their cybernetic humans function optimally.

Her mind was preoccupied with the process and dissecting what had gone differently with Hawk when klaxons blared, shattering the relative calm of the colony. Simone jerked upright from her workstation, heart pounding. Through the reinforced windows, she glimpsed the unmistakable silhouettes of Sventian warships descending upon them like a swarm of locusts.

"Vorn's launched his next attack." Tiberius's voice crackled over the comm, laced with urgency. "All personnel to battle stations immediately."

Simone's mind raced as she sprinted toward the command center, her lab coat billowing behind her. They'd anticipated this day, but the reality still struck like a blow to the gut. She burst into the war room, met by a flurry of activity.

"Sitrep?" Her clipped tone demanded an immediate update.

Tiberius, his cybernetic enhancements glinting under the harsh lights, straightened from the holographic display. His optic enhancement focused on her for a second as though scanning her. He probably was, wanting to reassure himself she wasn't about to faint with terror. "The Scourge has us surrounded on all fronts. They're pummeling our outer defenses with heavy artillery."

His expression hardened, a steely resolve etched into his features. "But they're about to face something they've never encountered before."

Simone felt a surge of pride mingled with unease. The biocircuit integration had unlocked unprecedented capabilities within Tiberius and the Iron Wolves, but its true potential remained untested in the crucible of battle.

"You're certain your team is prepared?" She searched his eyes.

Tiberius met her gaze fearlessly. "We were born ready." With a subtle nod, he signaled to his mercs, and they fanned out, assuming their positions with precision.

Simone watched, awestruck, as Tiberius seamlessly coordinated the defense efforts. His movements were a blur, his reflexes operating on a plane far beyond human limitations. He issued rapid-fire commands, his tactical acumen amplified by the neural interface's computational power.

Outside, the first wave of Sventian ground troops breached the perimeter, swarming toward the colony's heart. Simone's breath hitched as Tiberius and the Iron Wolves left the illusory safety of the command center and engaged the enemy, their cybernetic enhancements propelling them into a whirlwind of lethal efficiency.

Tiberius moved with a fluid grace that belied his imposing stature, his enhanced musculature and synthetic fibers granting him superhuman strength and speed. He deflected enemy fire with uncanny precision, his cybernetic eye tracking multiple targets simultaneously.

Beside him, Lancer's bionic arm transformed into a high-caliber cannon, raining a hailstorm of concentrated plasma bursts upon the advancing Sventian forces. Hawk soared overhead, her enhancements allowing her to jump so high and hover so long it gave the illusion of flight, allowing her to rain down suppressing fire from above while evading return volleys with ease.

Simone watched, transfixed, as the battle unfolded before her eyes. The Iron Wolves fought as a seamless unit, their neural interfaces enabling instantaneous coordination and shared tactical awareness.

"Come on," said Izzy, tugging at her arm. "We need to make sure the lab is secure."

"Of course." She followed her friend out of the command center, heading back to the lab. The Sventians had breached the building, and the battle raged around Simone as she sprinted through the smoke-filled corridors behind Izzy. Explosions rocked the colony, sending tremors through the floor beneath her feet. She stumbled, catching herself against the wall as debris rained down.

Somewhere behind her, the unmistakable sound of heavy footfalls echoed, drawing ever closer. Vorn's deep, guttural voice carried over the din, taunting her. "You can't escape me, Doctor."

Realizing he was there to hunt her made it far realer than it had been when she'd first heard the news he wanted revenge for her shooting him. In the haze of smoke, she lost track of Izzy and found herself running down a corridor that wasn't familiar, shrouded as it was in the haze.

"I've seen your pretty upgrades, and I want them and all the tech." His chilling words echoed from behind her.

Simone reached into her pocket to extract a laser scalpel she'd placed there earlier. It hadn't been intended to be a weapon, but it would have to do. Her grip tightened on the laser scalpel clutched in her hand. She refused to be taken, refused to let her life's work fall into the hands of that ruthless scourge.

Rounding a corner, she recognized where she was when the smoke cleared somewhat and was soon in the main laboratory, slipping through a maze of workstations and cutting-edge equipment. Her territory was now a potential trap. She darted behind a bank of computers, chest heaving as she fought to control her ragged breaths.

The doors hissed open, and Vorn's towering form filled the entrance, his cybernetic claw glinting menacingly. It looked so crude compared to the symmetrical beauty of the cybernetics the Iron Wolves bore. "Come out, come out, little scientist." His lips curled into a predatory smile. "I promise I'll make your death quick if you surrender peacefully."

Simone remained motionless, her mind racing. She had to buy time and hold out until Tiberius and the others could reach her.

"Your toys are impressive," Vorn said, stalking through the lab, his footsteps heavy and deliberate. "But they're nothing compared to the power you could wield at my side."

"I'd planned to kill you for what you did to me, but..." He paused, cocking his head as if listening for any telltale sound that might give away her location. "Join me, Dr. Wiley. Become my consort, and together, we'll reshape the galaxy in our image."

Simone clenched her jaw, revulsion churning in her gut. She would never submit to that monster while a single breath remained in her body.

Vorn's shadow loomed over her hiding spot. "Hello," he said with a wicked grin that held a menacing edge.

She tensed, preparing to strike.

"Don't be a fool," he said, sounding almost indulgent. "Your resistance only delays the inevitable. You will see to my enhancements, and you'll either come with me to serve my will, or your tech will, but you won't win against me."

His words irritated her, making her act rashly. In a blur of motion, Simone leapt from her cover, the laser scalpel raised high. Vorn's eyes widened in surprise.

Their gazes locked, and time seemed to slow. Simone saw the hunger in his eyes, the twisted desire to possess her, to break her will and bend her to his whims while turning her invention into a way to strengthen the Scourge and set them loose on the galaxy.

Never.

With a feral snarl, she brought the scalpel down in a vicious arc, aiming for his exposed throat. Vorn reacted with blinding speed, his cybernetic arm deflecting the blow with a resounding clang.

The impact jarred her bones, but she refused to relent. She pressed the attack, raining down a flurry of strikes, each one fueled by her determination to survive, to protect all she held dear, and to keep him from tapping into the power Tiberius and the others now had. His crude illegal enhancements were no match for what her tech could give him, and unleashing that kind of power through him on the world was abhorrent.

Vorn parried her blows, his laughter a deep rumble. "Such fire," he said with a vicious grin. "I'll enjoy breaking you."

Feinting left, Simone ducked under his guard and slashed at his midsection. The scalpel's searing beam sliced through his armor, drawing a thin line of viscous fluid.

Vorn roared in pain and rage, his fist lashing out and catching Simone squarely in the ribs. The force of the blow lifted her off her feet, sending her crashing into a nearby console. Stars danced across her vision as she crumpled to the floor, gasping for air. The scalpel clattered from her grasp, its beam sputtering out.

Vorn loomed over her, his expression twisted into a rictus of fury. "You'll pay for that." He reached down, his cybernetic claw extending toward her throat.

Simone's fingers scrabbled across the debris-strewn floor, seeking any weapon or means of defense. Her hand closed around a jagged shard of metal, and she gripped it tightly, bracing herself.

As Vorn's claw closed around her neck, she struck, driving the shard deep into the joint of his wrist, which was still fully biological, with every ounce of strength she could muster.

Vorn bellowed in agony, recoiling as blood spurted from the damaged limb. Simone seized the opportunity, rolling to her feet and snatching up the scalpel once more.

With a feral cry, she charged, the scalpel's beam flaring to life. Vorn turned, his remaining hand raised in a futile attempt to deflect her attack.

The searing blade sliced through his outstretched arm, cleaving it from his body in a shower of sparks and fluid. Vorn's agonized howls echoed through the lab as he staggered back, clutching the cauterized stump.

Simone stood her ground, the scalpel raised, chest heaving with exertion. "I'll never let you have my technology, Vorn," she shouted with defiance.

Before Vorn could respond, the doors burst open, and Tiberius stormed in, his cybernetic enhancements glowing with power. His gaze swept over the scene, taking in Simone's battered form and Vorn's grievous wounds. "Simone." His voice was both relief and fury as he crossed the distance in a blur of motion.

Vorn snarled, his remaining hand transforming into a wicked-looking blaster. "This isn't over, human."

Tiberius moved with superhuman speed, interposing himself between Simone and the Sventian leader. His cybernetic eye tracked Vorn's every twitch, his muscles coiled and ready to strike.

The deafening roar of battle faded into the background as Simone's world narrowed to the two towering figures before her. Tiberius, his cybernetic enhancements humming with power, stood ready, shielding her from Vorn's wrath.

Simone's breath caught in her throat as Tiberius shifted positions, his muscles coiling like taut cables, ready to strike. His optic implant tracking Vorn's every move as his reflexes operated on a plane far beyond human limitations.

In a blur of motion, Vorn raised his blaster, the muzzle glowing ominously. Simone's heart raced as her fingers tightened around the laser scalpel. She braced for the inevitable clash.

Tiberius's cybernetic arm lashed out, deflecting Vorn's first volley with a resounding clang that reverberated through the lab. Vorn snarled, his blaster arm recalibrating with lightning speed, unleashing a rapid-fire barrage of plasma bolts. Tiberius weaved and dodged, his enhanced agility allowing him to evade the lethal fusillade with ease.

Simone watched, terrified but unable to look away as the two clashed, their movements a dizzying dance of violence and precision. Tiberius pressed his advantage, raining down a flurry of blows that forced Vorn onto the defensive.

With a feral roar, Vorn lashed out, his cybernetic claw slicing through the air like a whip. Tiberius twisted, narrowly avoiding the strike, and countered with a vicious uppercut from his cyborg arm that struck the Sventian leader.

Vorn stumbled back, his blaster arm swinging wildly, unleashing a torrent of plasma fire that scorched the lab's walls. Simone flinched, ducking behind a console as shrapnel and sparks rained down around her.

Through the haze of smoke and debris, she glimpsed Tiberius closing in, his movements fluid and relentless. He battered Vorn's defenses, each blow landing with bone-jarring force.

Vorn's laughter echoed through the chaos, a deep, mocking rumble. "Is that all you've got, human? I expected more from the great Tiberius Peña."

Tiberius didn't rise to the taunt. He feinted left, then struck with blinding speed, his cybernetic fist slamming into Vorn's midsection with the force of a small artillery shell.

The impact lifted Vorn off his feet, sending him crashing through a bank of computers in a shower of sparks and twisted metal. Simone ducked instinctively as more debris rained down around her.

Vorn emerged from the wreckage, his armor rent and scorched, but his eyes burned with a maniacal gleam. "Not bad, human. I look forward to having your enhancements, but I'll be able to fully use them. You're too weak to have such a gift." With a flick of his wrist, a wicked-looking blade extended from his remaining cybernetic limb. He twirled the blade, his movements almost casual, as if taunting Tiberius to make the next move.

Simone's grip tightened on the laser scalpel. She knew better than to intervene. Tiberius's enhanced reflexes and combat prowess far outstripped her own, but every fiber of her being yearned to stand at his side, to face this threat together as partners.

As if sensing her thoughts, Tiberius glanced over his shoulder, his cybernetic eye locking with gaze. Tiberius gave her the slightest nod, a wordless reassurance, before turning his attention back to Vorn. His stance shifted, his body coiling as he prepared to engage once more.

Vorn charged, his blade a blur of lethal steel as he unleashed a whirlwind of strikes. Tiberius parried and deflected each blow, his movements a seamless fusion of raw power and calculated precision.

The two clashed in a whirlwind of violence, their enhanced forms striking with the force of colliding asteroids. Simone could only watch as the battle raged around her, having trouble keeping track of how fast they moved.

Tiberius seized an opening, his cybernetic fist slamming into Vorn's jaw with a sickening crunch. The Sventian leader staggered, his blade clattering to the floor as he fought to maintain his footing.

Seizing the advantage, Tiberius pressed his assault, raining down a relentless barrage of blows that battered Vorn's defenses. Each strike landed with bone-jarring force, the sound of rending metal echoing through the lab.

Vorn snarled, his remaining hand lashing out in a desperate bid to gain some respite. His cybernetic claw raked across Tiberius's chest, scoring deep furrows in his armor and drawing a thin line of blue fluid.

Tiberius grunted, his expression tightening with pain, but he refused to relent. With a feral roar, he unleashed a devastating uppercut that lifted Vorn off his feet, sending him crashing to the floor in a heap of twisted metal and sparking circuitry.

Silence descended over the lab, punctuated only by the crackle of exposed wiring and the ragged sound of Vorn's labored breathing. Simone emerged from her cover, her heart pounding in her ears as she approached Tiberius.

He turned to face her, his cybernetic enhancements still glowing with power, his expression a mix of triumph and concern. Without a word, he pulled her into a fierce embrace, his arms enveloping her in a protective cocoon.

Simone melted into Tiberius's embrace, drawing strength from the solidity of his form, the reassuring thrum of his cybernetic enhancements. His arms enveloped her, a protective cocoon shielding her from the chaos that raged around them.

For a fleeting moment, the sounds of battle faded into the background, replaced by the steady beat of his heart, and the rhythmic whir of his synthetic components. Simone reveled in his presence and the certainty he would always stand at her side, no matter the odds.

All too soon, the respite shattered as a thunderous explosion rocked the colony, jolting them back to the grim reality they faced. Tiberius's grip tightened, his body tensing as he scanned the smoke-filled lab for any lingering threats.

"We need to regroup," he said, his voice a low rumble that reverberated through her bones. "The others will be converging on our position."

Simone nodded, reluctantly extricating herself from his embrace. Her fingers trailed along the scorched furrows in his armor.

As if sensing her thoughts, Tiberius caught her hand, his cybernetic eye locking with her gaze. "We'll be okay."

His conviction bolstered her resolve, and she squared her shoulders, pushing aside the lingering tendrils of fear. "I know," she said, her voice steadier than she had anticipated.

The sound of approaching footsteps drew their attention, and Simone turned to see Lance and the others emerging from the smoke-filled corridors. Their armor bore the scars of battle, but their eyes burned with a fierce determination that mirrored Tiberius's own.

"Status report," said Tiberius, his tone all business as he slipped seamlessly into his role as commander.

Lancer stepped forward, his expression grim. "The outer defenses have been breached, but we've managed to contain the Sventian forces within the secondary perimeter. For now."

His gaze flicked toward the twisted heap of metal and sparking circuitry that had once been Vorn. "Their leader is down, but they're regrouping under a new command structure."

Tiberius's jaw tightened, his cybernetic eye flickering as he processed the information. "We need to press our advantage while we still can. Hawk, what's our aerial situation?"

The lithe sniper stepped forward. "The skies are clear for now, but they've got heavy artillery inbound. We'll need to neutralize those cannons before they can bring them to bear."

Tiberius nodded, his expression grim. "That's our priority. Lance, take Brick and secure the artillery emplacements. Hawk, provide overwatch and take out any stragglers."

His gaze shifted to Simone, and she saw a flicker of concern cross his features. "You should retreat to the secure bunker until we've regained control of the situation."

Simone opened her mouth to protest, but he raised a hand, his expression brooking no argument. "I can't afford any distractions, Simone. Worrying about you could get me killed."

She wanted to argue, to insist on standing by his side, but his words gave her pause. This wasn't about her pride or her desire to contribute. This was about ensuring the survival of everything they had built, of every life that depended on their success.

With a reluctant nod, she acquiesced, tightening her fingers around the laser scalpel still clutched in her hand. "Be careful out there," she said, her voice thick with emotion.

Tiberius's expression softened, and he reached out, his cybernetic hand cupping her cheek in a tender gesture. "Always," he promised. With a sharp nod to his team, he turned and strode from the lab, his movements purposeful and determined. Simone watched him go, her heart swelling with pride and fear.

As the sound of their footsteps faded, she was alone in the ravaged laboratory, surrounded by the twisted wreckage of their battle with Vorn. She cast a glance at the Sventian leader's motionless form, her lip curling in disgust.

A flicker of movement caught her eye, and she tensed, her grip tightening on the scalpel as she scanned the shadows for any lingering threats. A low groan echoed through the stillness, and she zeroed in on the source—a crumpled figure half-buried beneath a pile of debris.

Cautiously, she approached, her steps light and measured. As she drew closer, she recognized the battered form of Izzy, her friend's face streaked with soot and blood.

"Izzy." Simone dropped to her knees beside the other woman, fingers fumbling for a pulse. Relief washed over her as she felt the steady thrum of life beneath her fingertips.

Izzy's eyes fluttered open, her gaze unfocused and dazed. "S-Simone?" Her voice was a ragged whisper, laced with pain.

"I'm here," Simone soothed, her hands already working to clear the debris pinning her friend. "Just hold on, okay? I've got you."

With a grunt of effort, she heaved aside a twisted slab of metal, freeing Izzy from the wreckage. The other woman cried out, her face contorting in agony as Simone gently eased her onto her back.

Simone's breath caught in her throat as she took in the extent of Izzy's injuries. A jagged shard of shrapnel protruded from her abdomen, her blood seeping in a steady crimson flow.

"Oh, Izzy..." Simone's voice wavered, her hands hovering uncertainly over the grievous wound.

Izzy's fingers closed around her wrist, her grip surprisingly strong despite her condition. "Don't...give me that look," she said, her lips quirking in a ghost of a smile. "I've...had worse."

Simone chuckled even as tears stung her eyes. Trust Izzy to maintain her sense of humor, even in the direst of circumstances.

Steeling herself, Simone reached for the medkit tucked into the pocket of her lab coat. "Just hold still," she said, her fingers deftly retrieving the necessary supplies. "This is going to hurt, but I'll be as gentle as I can."

She set about stemming the flow of blood and stabilizing Izzy's condition. Her hands moved with a steady surety born of years of experience, her focus narrowing to the task at hand.

As she worked, Izzy's gaze remained fixed on her, her eyes shining with pain and a surprising amount of cheer. "You always...did have a way...with sharp objects," she quipped, her voice strained.

Simone smiled as she applied the final dressing to Izzy's wound. "And you always did have a knack for finding trouble," she retorted, her tone laced with affection.

Izzy's laughter dissolved into a fit of coughing, her body wracked with spasms of pain. Simone's heart clenched, and she reached out, her fingers brushing the sweat-dampened strands of hair from Izzy's brow.

"Easy," she soothed, her voice a gentle murmur. "Save your strength. You're going to be just fine."

Izzy's eyes fluttered open, her gaze locking with Simone's. "You know…that's not true," she whispered, her words laced with a finality that sent a chill down Simone's spine.

"Don't say that," Simone chided, her voice wavering despite her best efforts to maintain her composure. "We've been through worse scrapes than this, remember? That time on Arcadia Prime when we –"

"Simone." Izzy's fingers tightened around her wrist, her grip insistent. "Listen to me."

Simone fell silent, her throat constricting as she met Izzy's unwavering gaze.

"You're going to have to upgrade me if I'm going to live. Make me a cyborg."

She didn't hesitate as she gently lifted Izzy onto the metal console closest to the equipment. There was no biobed operating, so it was riskier than the others' conversions, but this was Izzy's only chance.

The makeshift operating table gleamed under the harsh laboratory lights, casting eerie shadows across Izzy's pale face. Her hands trembled as she reached for the biocircuit interface, the decision pressing down on her like a physical force. "Are you sure about this?" asked Simone.

Izzy's eyes fluttered open, a weak smile tugging at her lips. "Do I have a choice?" She coughed, a wet, rattling sound that made Simone's stomach clench. "Besides, I always wanted to be part robot. Think of the pranks I could pull."

Despite the gravity of the situation, she chuckled. "Only you could joke at a time like this." She took a deep breath, steadying her nerves as she began the delicate process of integrating the biocircuit interface with Izzy's nervous system.

The room filled with the soft hum of machinery, and the steady beep of medical monitors.

As Simone worked, her mind raced through calculations and procedures. She had to be precise, meticulous, and work without the biobed keeping Izzy in perfect homeostasis. One wrong move could spell disaster. The responsibility pressed down on her, threatening to crush her.

"Talk to me," said Izzy, her voice strained. "Distract me."

Simone nodded, her eyes never leaving her work as she started speaking. "Remember that time on Epsilon Prime? When we sneaked into the restricted zone to study those bioluminescent fungi?"

Izzy's laugh turned into a pained groan. "How could I forget? You tripped and fell face-first into a patch of spores. Your skin glowed for a week."

"I looked like a human nightlight," said Simone, carefully attaching neural connectors to Izzy's cerebral cortex. "The looks I got in the cafeteria were priceless."

"Not as priceless as the look on Professor Hadley's face when you showed up to give your presentation," said Izzy. "I thought his eyes were going to pop out of his head."

The conversation flowed between them, a lifeline of normalcy in the chaos. Simone's hands moved with precision, her focus absolute as she integrated synthetic components with organic tissue.

Hours passed in a blur of intense concentration and delicate maneuvering. Simone's back ached from hunching over the makeshift operating table, but she refused to stop. Izzy's life hung in the balance, and she wouldn't fail her friend.

As the final connections were made, Simone stepped back, her breath catching in her throat. Izzy lay motionless on the console, her body a hybrid of flesh and machine. The biocircuit interface pulsed with a soft, blue light, syncing with Izzy's vital signs and forming small, visible webbing in lines throughout her skull.

"Izzy?" Simone called softly, her heart pounding. "Can you hear me?"

For a long, agonizing moment, there was no response. Slowly, Izzy's eyes opened. The ocular implant glowed with an otherworldly blue light. " This is amazing."

Simone sagged with relief. "How do you feel?"

Izzy flexed her fingers, watching as synthetic muscles rippled beneath her skin. "Like I could bench press a spaceship." She paused, her brow furrowing. "But also like I might throw up. Is that normal?"

"Your system is still adjusting." Simone ran a diagnostic scan. "It'll take some time for everything to fully integrate, but your results are nominal."

As she spoke, the lab doors hissed open. Tiberius strode in, his cybernetic enhancements still glowing from recent combat. His eyes widened as he took in the scene before him. "What have you done?"

Simone straightened, squaring her shoulders. "What I had to do to save her life."

"I can see that." He approached cautiously, his gaze fixed on Izzy's newly augmented form. "Is she...stable?"

"Hey, I'm right here," said Izzy, slowly sitting up. "And I'm fine. Well, mostly fine. A little nauseated and kind of buzzy, but fine."

Tiberius nodded, a hint of approval in his expression. "Impressive work, considering the circumstances." He turned to Simone, his face softening. "We've done it. The Sventian Scourge has been defeated."

Relief washed over Simone, threatening to buckle her knees. "It's over?"

"Not entirely. There are still pockets of resistance, but their main force has been routed. Vorn is dead, and their fleet is in disarray."

Simone closed her eyes, allowing herself a moment to absorb the news. When she opened them, she found Tiberius watching her intently.

"You should rest," he said softly. "You've been through hell."

She shook her head. "Not yet. I need to monitor Izzy's integration process. Make sure there are no complications."

Tiberius stepped closer, his hand coming to rest on her shoulder. The warmth of his touch seeped through her, a stark contrast to the cold metal of the lab. "You've done enough for now," he said, his voice gentle but firm. "Let the medical team and Dr. Valeria take over. You need to recharge."

Simone wanted to argue, but exhaustion weighed heavily on her. She glanced at Izzy, who gave her a reassuring nod.

"Go," said Izzy. "I promise not to turn into a homicidal cyborg while you're gone. Well...probably not."

Despite everything, Simone laughed. "All right, but I'll be back soon to check on you."

As she allowed Tiberius to lead her from the lab, she cast one last glance at Izzy. Her friend waved, the gesture slightly jerky as she adjusted to her new cybernetic enhancements.

The corridor outside was a flurry of activity, personnel rushing back and forth as they dealt with the aftermath of the battle. Simone leaned against Tiberius, suddenly aware of how drained she truly was.

"Come on," he said, steering her toward her quarters. "You need to rest."

She nodded, too tired to argue. As they walked, her thoughts drifted to the future. The Sventian Scourge was defeated, but at what cost? And what would this mean for their colony?

She pushed aside the thoughts, focusing on the steady rhythm of his footsteps beside her. For now, they were alive. They had survived. Everything else could wait until she had slept.

As they reached her quarters, Tiberius paused, his hand hovering over the door controls. "Simone," he said, his voice low and intense. "What you did back there, with Izzy, all by yourself, was incredible."

She looked up at him, confused by the admiration in his eyes. "I did what I had to do," she said simply.

He nodded, a small smile playing at the corners of his mouth. "That's what makes you so remarkable." He leaned in, pressing a gentle kiss to her forehead. "Get some rest. I'll be here when you wake up."

As she entered her quarters, the door sliding shut behind her, she found herself smiling despite her exhaustion. They had faced impossible odds and come out the other side. She collapsed onto her bed, her body finally giving in to the bone-deep weariness that had been building for hours. As she drifted off to sleep, her last thoughts were of Tiberius, of Izzy, and of the strange, wonderful family they had forged.

116

Chapter 10—Tiberius

IN THE AFTERMATH OF the battle, Izzy and the med techs worked tirelessly to save those they could. Simone's fledgling cybernetics technology proved invaluable, allowing Izzy to stabilize the critically injured and enhance their chances of survival.

Tiberius watched in awe as they moved from one patient to the next for hours. When Simone slipped out to stand with him on the surface, he put his arm around her. "They've been employing your tech for hours to save lives."

She scowled. "You should have woken me to help." Without another word, she rushed to join the team, her hands steady and her focus unwavering. She integrated the biocircuit interface with precision, her brilliant mind guiding the delicate procedure.

Tiberius marveled at her strength and dedication before refocusing the mercs to finish triaging and then to start on the daunting task of clearing up all the debris from the battle. They would have a lot of rebuilding before them, but most of them were alive to make it happen, which was amazing considering the might of the Sventians.

AS THE HOURS STRETCHED into days, the medbay became a hive of activity, with Simone at its center. She worked tirelessly, her fingers flying over consoles and surgical tools with equal dexterity.

Tiberius was drawn to her side, offering what support he could as she and Izzy directed the operation and focused on healing everyone who was injured in order of severity. He assisted in the procedures, his enhanced strength and dexterity proving invaluable, but more than that, he provided a steadying presence.

As the last of the survivors stabilized, Tiberius, Simone, and Izzy finally allowed themselves a moment of rest. Izzy wished them well and promised to see them after sleeping for a decade, at least. In turn, they retreated to the quiet of Simone's quarters, their bodies weary but spirits unbroken.

Simone sank onto the bed, her eyes heavy with fatigue. "We did it, Tiberius. We saved as many as we could."

Tiberius settled beside her, his cybernetic arm wrapping around her shoulders. "Because of you," he said, his voice thick with emotion.

Simone shook her head, a faint smile playing on her lips. "We did it together. You and the Iron Wolves gave us the chance to fight back. Without your bravery and tactical genius, none of this would have been possible."

Tiberius tightened his embrace, drawing her closer. "Izzy did her fair share too. She seems to like being a cyborg."

Simone's eyes glistened with amusement. "I wish she'd make fewer jokes about going homicidal and enslaving the human race though."

He laughed. "She's probably joking. Right?"

She shrugged but was grinning. "Maybe."

Tiberius leaned in, his forehead resting against hers. He felt a sense of completeness, a certainty that their paths had been destined to intertwine. "I love you," he said, his heart swelling with an amount of love he had never known possible.

She laid her head against his shoulder, yawning deeply before she said, "Love you too."

As they held each other, the weight of their losses and the challenges that lay ahead seemed to fade into the background. For now, they slumped together on the bed and slept.

IN THE DAYS THAT FOLLOWED, Tiberius was swept up in the colony's renewed energy. Everywhere he turned, he witnessed the indomitable spirit of the survivors, their determination to rebuild and thrive fueling their every action.

One evening, as the twin moons of Durmox C7 cast their ethereal glow over the courtyard, Tiberius was drawn to a gathering of colonists. They sat around a crackling fire, sharing stories and laughter, their faces illuminated by the dancing flames.

As Tiberius approached, he recognized the familiar voice of Lance, one of the Iron Wolves. The mercenary was regaling the group with a tale from their days in the interstellar military, his words painting a vivid picture of a daring raid on a pirate stronghold.

"We were outnumbered ten to one, but Tiberius had a plan. A crazy, audacious plan that no sane person would have even considered."

The colonists leaned forward, enraptured by the story. Tiberius felt a pang of nostalgia, remembering the bond he had forged with his comrades in those days, a bond that had only strengthened over time.

He didn't miss the way Izzy moved closer to Lance as his second-in-command spoke, and how Lance casually took her hand. It seemed like there were all kinds of new bonds being forged, which made him smile.

Lance continued, his voice rising and falling with the cadence of a seasoned storyteller. "We infiltrated their base under the cover of darkness, moving like ghosts through their defenses, and then, just as the sun began to rise, Tiberius gave the signal."

He paused for dramatic effect, his gaze sweeping over the rapt audience. "In a blaze of plasma fire and shrapnel, we struck. The thieves never knew what hit them. By the time the smoke cleared, we had secured the base and captured their leader."

A chorus of cheers and applause erupted from the colonists, their faces aglow with admiration. Tiberius was proud, not just of the victory itself, but for the camaraderie it represented.

As the applause died down, a young colonist, her eyes wide with wonder, turned to Tiberius. "Is it true, Commander? Did you really pull off such a daring raid?"

Tiberius allowed a rare smile to tug at the corners of his mouth. "The details may have been embellished slightly," he said, his voice carrying a hint of amusement, "But the essence of the story is true. We faced overwhelming odds, but we never lost faith in each other or in our mission."

The young colonist nodded, her expression one of reverence. "You're a hero, Commander," she said, her voice filled with admiration.

Tiberius shook his head, his expression growing solemn. "The true heroes are those who made the ultimate sacrifice," he said, his thoughts turning to his comrades and the colonists they had lost recently and over the years. "We honor their memory by continuing to fight for a better future."

A hush fell over the gathering. In that moment, they were united in celebration and solemn remembrance of those who had fallen. Tiberius felt Simone's presence before he saw her, her familiar warmth enveloping him like a gentle embrace. She stepped into the circle of firelight, her eyes shining with pride and determination.

"My father had a vision," she said, her voice carrying a quiet strength that commanded attention. "He believed this colony could be a place where science and innovation could flourish, unencumbered by the constraints and corruption of the Coalition. We have endured hardships that would have broken lesser souls, but we persevered, and in doing so, we have proven ourselves worthy of carrying on my father's legacy."

She paused, her gaze sweeping over the gathered colonists. "The road ahead won't always be easy. We'll face obstacles, setbacks, and perhaps even more battles, but we'll face them together, as a united front, driven by a shared vision of a better tomorrow."

A murmur of agreement rippled through the crowd.

Tiberius felt a surge of pride and purpose, his cybernetic enhancements thrumming with energy. As Simone's words faded into the night, the colonists erupted into thunderous applause, their spirits buoyed by her vision and their shared resolve.

He reached out to hold Simone's hand. Together, they were unstoppable—a force of nature, driven by love, courage, and commitment to create a better world.

Tiberius pulled Simone into his embrace, the warmth of her body seeping into his cybernetically-enhanced form. He claimed her in a searing kiss, conveying the depth of his love and devotion. For a moment, the world around them seemed to fade away, leaving only the two of them, united in their shared passion and purpose.

As they parted, breathless, he gazed into her eyes. "I love you, Simone."

Simone's fingers traced the contours of his face, her touch gentle yet electrifying. "I love you, Tiberius," she said, her voice thick with emotion.

As the celebration continued around them, he was drawn into the revelry once more. He laughed and danced alongside his comrades, his cybernetic enhancements allowing him to move with a grace and fluidity that sometimes still made him stop and marvel at what he could do now.

Simone watched him with amusement and adoration, her eyes sparkling with a joy. Izzy whispered something to her before disappearing with Lance. He shared a knowing look with her, and they both grinned as he leaned closer while the celebration continued.

Through it all, Simone was by his side, her presence a constant source of strength and inspiration. In her eyes, he saw the future they were building together—a future that awed and humbled him while leaving him anxious to experience every moment of it with her.

About Juno

JUNO WELLS GREW UP on Florida's Space Coast, watching the shuttles take off from Cape Canaveral. When she hit college, her childhood fantasies about space travel turned highly romantic. Now her mind reels with space adventures of fantastic alien lords in distant galaxies, and the earth women they love.

Wells' stories explore the complex, sensual relationships between inhabitants of different star systems. There are always happy endings just as there is always a new world to explore.

Have a comment? Make first contact with Juno at authorjunowells@gmail.com.

Get her newsletter: subscribeto.eo.page/junowells (Get a free book!)

About Aurelia

AURELIA SKYE IS THE pen name Kit Tunstall uses when writing science fiction romance. It's simply a way to separate the myriad types of stories she writes so readers know what to expect with each "author."

USA Today Bestselling author Kit Tunstall lives in the Midwest with her husband and two sons. She enjoys writing several genres and subgenres, but almost everything she writes has a strong romantic element.

<u>Website</u>[1]

---

1. http://www.kittunstall.com

Did you love *Cyborgs' Origin*? Then you should read *Alien Baby Pact Compilation* by Aurelia Skye and Juno Wells!

Seven years ago, the Faction agreed to save Earth from the vorathan invasion in exchange for Earth women giving them one year of proxy rights to act as a surrogate, since the aliens of the Faction faced a dwindling population. With the vorathans feared throughout the galaxy as bloodthirsty, vicious marauders, the Earth's government agreed.

That doesn't mean the women did.

This is a compilation of all seven stories in the series.

Sometimes, you want to read about the entire alien empire and all its myriad twists and turns, immersing yourself in hundreds of pages of intrigue. And sometimes, you want to skip the frills and get to the main event. Juno and Aurelia are pleased to bring you a series of short, steamy romances about untouched human women making babies with their truly alien mates.

Also by Aurelia Skye

Alien Baby Pact
Baby For The Brundle Commander
Baby For The Serp General
Alien Baby Pact Compilation
Baby For The Grimlock General
Baby For The Palantir Chief
Baby For The Alphan Captain
Baby For The Mosaic Med Chief
Baby For The Tark Commander

Alien Baby Pakt
Alien Baby Pakt Zusammenstellung

BioCircuit Nexus
Cyborgs' Origin

Celestial Mates
Wrong Place, Right Mate
Destined For The Drakari Warlords

Cybernetic Hearts
Mated To The Cyborg General
Claimed By The Cyborg Commander
Fated For The Cyborg Officer
Meant For The Cyborg Captain
Baby For The Cyborg General
Cybernetic Hearts: Complete Series

Dazon Agenda
Written In The Stars
Alien's Babies
Diplomatic Affairs
Moon Madness
Across The Stars
Emperor's Assassin Bride
Dazon Agenda: Complete Collection
Compilation de l'Agenda Dazon

Future Fairytales
Hooked

Guerriers Blessés
Chassé
Inlassable
Marqué
Justice
Compilation Guerriers Blessés

Harrow Bay
Hell Gates & Hot Flashes
Nightmares & Night Sweats
Warlocks & Wrinkles
Love Spells & Liver Spots
Phantasms & Presbyopia
Vampires & Varicose Veins
Mermaids & Mood Swings
Séances & Sagging Skin
Necromancy & Knee Pains
Marids & Memory Loss
Devil Deals & Dizzy Spells
Happy Endings & New Beginnings
Harrow Bay, Volume 1
Hellhounds & Mistletoe
Harrow Bay, Volume 2
Harrow Bay, Volume 3
Harrow Bay Complete Series

Harrow Bucht Serie
Höllentore & Hitzewallungen
Alpträume Und Nachtschweiß
Hexenmeister & Falten
Liebeszauber Und Leberflecken
Phantasmen Und Alterssichtigkeit
Vampire und Krampfadern
Meerjungfrauen Und Stimmungsschwankungen
Séancen Und Schlaffe Haut
Nekromantie Und Knieschmerzen
Marids und Gedächtnisverlust
Teufelsgeschäfte Und Schwindelzauber
Happy Ends Und Neuanfängen
Höllenhunde & Mistelzweige

Hell Virus
Catching Hell
Surviving Hell
Bleeding Hell
Raising Hell
Sharing Hell

Howls Romance
The Jaguar Alpha's Forbidden Lover
CEO Wolf Shifter's Surprise Twins

Northstar Shifters
Northstar Heir's Scarred Mate

Olympus Station
Station Commander's Surrogate
Alien Prince's Secret Baby
Security Agent's Alien Bartender
Olympus Station Compilation

SpicyShorts
Music In My Heart
Kilted Tentacle Monster: A Search for True Love

Sweet Escapes
Hook & Wendy

The Haunting of Clara Gray
Ghostly Awakening
Ghostly Harmonies

Three Crones Inn
Vastly Inn-proved
Ghastly Intentions
Grave Inn-tervention
Ghostly Inn-heritance
Three Crones Inn Compilation

True North
True North #1: Death & Deception
True North #2: Rescued & Revelations
True North #3: Fire & Ice
True North #4: Enemies & Lovers
True North #5: Truth & Tiranog
True North #6: Fight & Flight
True North #7: Love & Loss

Wounded Warriors
Relentless
Marked
Justice
Wounded Warriors Collection
Hunted

Standalone

Reluctant Companion
Princess By Mistake
Fire Lord's Assistant
True North
Dragon Laird's Witch
Alien General's Rebel Consort
Tempted By Demons
Enemy Combatant
Grotesquerie
Mistaken Bounty
Wahre Richtung
Power Surges & Amorous Urges
Taken By The Orc General
Compilation Alien Baby Pact

Also by Juno Wells

Alien Baby Pact
Baby For The Brundle Commander
Baby For The Serp General
Alien Baby Pact Compilation
Baby For The Grimlock General
Baby For The Palantir Chief
Baby For The Alphan Captain
Baby For The Mosaic Med Chief
Baby For The Tark Commander

Alien Baby Pakt
Alien Baby Pakt Zusammenstellung

BioCircuit Nexus
Cyborgs' Origin

Dazon Agenda
Written In The Stars
Alien's Babies
Diplomatic Affairs
Moon Madness
Across The Stars
Emperor's Assassin Bride
Dazon Agenda: Complete Collection
Compilation de l'Agenda Dazon

Galactic Alphas
Alpha's Omega
Buying His Omega
Claiming His Omega
Galactic Alphas Compilation

Standalone
Alien General's Rebel Consort
Compilation Alien Baby Pact

www.ingramcontent.com/pod-product-compliance
Lightning Source LLC
Chambersburg PA
CBHW071318130726
47996CB00002B/524